AF432867

Other Stories by Tim Niederriter

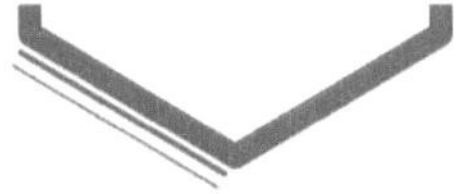

<u>Series Science Fiction and Fantasy</u>
Tenlyres
Spells of the Curtain
The Pillar Universe
Demon Hunter
<u>Other Stories</u>
Stolen Parts
Rem's Dream
Invisibles: Dark Work
Find all Tim's books and serials at www.mentalcellarpublications.com

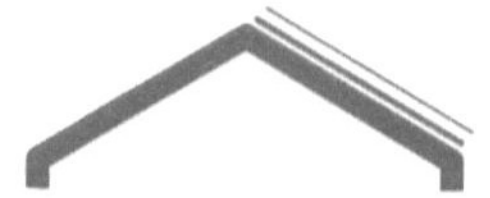

This series is for Peggy, my first great fan.

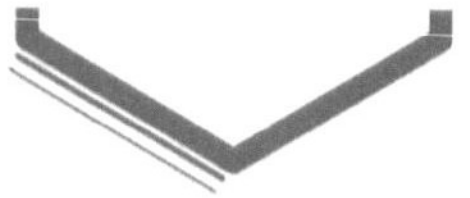

The Mangrove Suite
The Rain Protocol: Book One
By Tim Niederriter

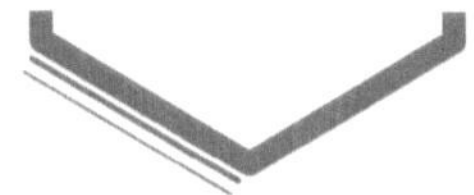

1

THE METRO'S MAIN CANAL sparkled with light as the ferry carried my friend Thomas and I down the waterway just after daybreak. Sunlight, I reminded myself, is no more real than the light veins provided by the governing aeons, though the sun has been around longer. I stood at the bow of the ferry, watching the water in the cold light of autumn. There was no ice on the canal yet, but even with my heavy overcoat and the stubborn fat around my gut, I felt a bit of a chill from the approaching winter.

We passed a large garden ringed by trees which bordered the canal, probably one belonging to a local aeon. Concealing foliage remained on the outside, but most of the leaves had turned red or orange already. Deeper inside the garden a glimmer of green confirmed my guess it belonged to an aeon. The central trees of an aeon's garden stayed both green and in flower longer than other trees. It also reminded me of the valley where I grew up, far west of the megalopolis.

I yawned, one hand in front of my mouth. Thomas insisted we leave early before the sun rose where we lived in the eastern city. Regardless of those plans, I had been up much of the night talking with Elizabeth about our strategy to break out with our own private network. I was tired. Elizabeth had a way of getting me focused on the future.

Just like when we had initially planned to live together four years ago. Even after our romantic relationship ended we remained each other's' best hope for striking it rich. From our positions with existing networks, the two of us could become the first mental network not run by aeons higher up, though someone would still have to invest in us, of course.

Thomas walked along the side of the ferry, a piece of toast in one hand and a thermos of coffee in the other. He looked as he always did, in a bit better shape than me and about the same height, dark hair and pale skin with black-rimmed glasses. He wore a small beard, which already showed a few strands of gray, and a dark coat. He stuffed the toast into his mouth and put his hand on the railing as he chewed.

I glanced at him. "Getting ready for a big buy?"

Thomas chewed a little more and then swallowed. "We'll see," he said, "but the right goods have to be there, or I won't buy."

The goods he referred to had once been people, but I never mentioned that to him anymore. Besides, they were all clean. Human slavery was wiped out over two hundred years ago. The aeons would not have allowed it once they took control of the cities, regardless. But cleans weren't people, however human they might appear.

I nodded. "Didn't you hire the ferry for a round trip?"

Thomas smirked. "I have a good feeling about the market today."

"Where'd you get the tip?"

He grinned. "Jeth, I'd almost think you were ready to get into this business."

"No way." I smelled the coffee as he unscrewed the lid and let steam waft out of his thermos.

"Not a chance? You mean even once you and Elizabeth have your new network set up?"

I shrugged. "It's not just because I don't have the money."

He looked out over the water, avoiding my eyes. "They creep you out, don't they? The cleans?"

"Isn't it kind of strange, how they look at you?"

Thomas took a sip from his thermos. "It's too early in the morning for this conversation."

"Sorry," I said.

"Never mind. Just take your ichor and you'll cheer up."

"You know I don't drink ichor on my days off."

"No wonder you're so grumpy. You cut your own network. How demanding is making shows all week?"

"It's not that." My job as a memeotect mostly involved building network programs like the old world's television programs but for projection directly into people's minds. "I've seen the problems with overusing ichor. That's all."

He got a far off, clouded look in his eyes as he accessed a network, telling me implicitly *he* had definitely taken a dose of ichor that morning. Thomas only connected for a moment. He disconnected and his eyes returned to normal. "One dose a day isn't gonna get you cleaned, you know?"

I shook my head. "I don't think like that. But I've seen too many people overdo it." Like Rebecca, from back home in the Green Valley. I hoped the signs of memories of the girl I once thought I loved didn't register on my face.

"Some day you're gonna have to tell me why you're so conservative."

"Maybe I will. Someday." Too much ichor could be poison to the mind even if it didn't transform you into a literal monster. And it did turn humans into beasts if overused.

"But not today, grumpy guts. I got it." Thomas turned from the water but then paused. "If they bother you that much, you didn't have to come with me."

I smiled out over the lapping waters of the bright canal. "We haven't seen each other enough lately."

"True that," he said. "But you can come upstairs and play cards any night. Elizabeth probably wouldn't mind that every now and then. Shit, man, you two can't work every night, am I right?"

"We're preparing for a network launch, but I see what you mean. I'll clear a time."

"Glad to hear it." He walked back down the length of the ferry. When he neared the tower that formed the helm, he turned and called out to me, "Looks like we'll be there in a few minutes."

I looked up from the water and glimpsed the dock carved into the side of the canal's concrete wall. "Got it," I called back. The sun poured down over the megalopolis, making skyscrapers gleam and shine. To the west the slender citadel towers of Aeon Heights rose even higher than the buildings constructed below for ordinary citizens, catching more than their share of sunlight. I turned from their brilliance and walked down the ferry's length to the raised bridge where Thomas waited to disembark.

THE MARKET ON THE SOUTH side of the canal was alive with countless people and cleans. Thomas and I arrived at the far end of the line and made our way along it to the mouth of the large auditorium repossessed from some sports team of times past. It now served as the showing area of the market. I didn't like the overall feel of the place. The veins that lined the ceiling glowed too bright in unhealthy white, and the cleans wore gaudy clothing that dazzled with reds and pinks and yellows.

Thomas marched down the center of our line into the mess of twirling, dancing cleans who displayed bodies perfected by pure endorphin-hunting days where nothing else mattered but the pleasure of the moment. I followed him, trying to remember why I had wanted to come to this place, even with a friend. We passed near-naked men and women with figures in suits hunched around them, inspecting nooks and crannies, cleans being examined by potential buyers.

I tried not to imagine Thomas doing the same thing because I didn't want to hate him. I didn't mean to hate him. What I wanted at that moment was to be anywhere but there. As if on cue, he stopped ten meters ahead of me and turned to a seller with two scantily clad women on either side of him. I made a face and turned to look into the center of the room where the dancers twirled and cavorted.

In the center of the dance, a woman whirled in a violet gown with a skirt riding high on her thighs and a trailing strand of golden cloth, flowing from her hair. Her skin was dark, though not as dark as mine, and perfect in the lights falling from the ceiling. I watched her enraptured for a moment, forgetting where I was. She reminded me of times past, back before I came to the megalopolis.

Back in the Green Valley. Years ago. Back with Rebecca, before she left to travel to the east.

Then my eyes narrowed. That dark haired, fine-skinned woman... eyes closed in gentle concentration, one leg raised in a frozen-seeming spin, was more than familiar to me.

"It can't be," I said under my breath. *Rebecca, what has become of you?*

No one paid any heed to my words. I took a step from the path, leaving Thomas to his business. Things needed to be seen. The truth needed to be found. Rebecca had probably been an addict of ichor when she left the valley, but what could have happened to her to place her among the cleans?

Could this really be her? I stood for what felt like several minutes, gazing at her, then tore my eyes away. After more than twelve years, she looked almost exactly as I remembered, sleek limbs and perfect curves. I fought the urge to return to staring, and instead, directed my attention to searching for Thomas. I had to tell someone.

A giant man stood beside the market stall closest to where Rebecca danced. As he talked to a buyer his massive arms folded, muscles rippling beneath the tattoos of intertwined snakes on both arms. My eyes passed over him twice before I realized the snakes on his arms had fanged, eyeless mouths on both ends.

Part of me knew not to feel intimidated by the giant's fearsome appearance. Another part of me did not like the idea of talking to him without knowing more about the woman on the stage. No matter how much she looked like Rebecca, the vast population of the megalopolis made it impossible for me to be certain she was really the girl I had known as a young man in the Green Valley. Without ichor, though, I had no networking ability so I could not even begin to search for any information I could use to identify Rebecca.

I glimpsed Thomas moving through the crowd a way down the path from me. He might have some ichor left from his morning. Most people carried a flask of it with them if they had business to attend to, and his management of the Mangrove Suite put him in demand during the day even when out on other business. I slipped through the crowd and caught up with Thomas.

"There you are, Jeth." He grinned. "I thought you might have gotten lost."

"Thomas, do you have any ichor left?"

"Woah, man. What happened?"

"I need to use the network."

"Sorry. I'm out, but there should be a supplier here you can buy a few drops from."

"Thanks. I'm going to go look."

"First of all, tell me what happened. I thought you didn't use on your off days?"

I shook my head. "I need to find something out. I'll tell you later."

"Alright." He nodded. His eyes seemed understanding despite his confusion. "I'll be making my way around the market. The ferry leaves a little after nightfall."

"Okay," I said. "I'll make sure I catch up with you before that." I turned and went back down the path toward the exit, my eyes peeled and searching for someone hawking ichor.

AEONS PRODUCE ICHOR, and they give it to the humans under their management. That's the most common way to get ichor in the megalopolis, but because the city is divided into the domains of different aeons there are other ways for those away from home. Vendors, like the one I found in the outer circle a few dozen yards from the entrance, filled that role in the market. For a price.

The vendor wore a heavy coat and stood by a low cart that carried a cooler. A security officer stood off to one side, bulletproof vest, triangular badge, but no visible weapons. This kind of vendor usually paid for extra security, and it looked like it cost her a hefty amount of credit. The vendor's hair was long and frizzy, and though the aeons kept most people in good health, she hunched, looking old and weary despite her smooth features.

She nodded to me, teeth bared in a grimy smile as I approached. "You need some ichor, sir?"

"Yes," I said. "How much for a single dose?"

"You from the canal districts?" she asked.

"Lotdel Tower. East of here."

"Canal. Got it. Fifty for a dose."

"Sounds reasonable."

The vendor held out her hand. "Show me some cred, and I'll hook you up."

"Thanks." I dropped my card into her palm. The card's light cell glowed in the dimness away from the central market lights. She swiped it on the side of her cooler and it opened a crack. Then she returned my card and lifted the cooler's lid. Golden liquid in clear plastic bags topped by sealed tubes that when opened could be used to drink the precious contents, lined the cooler. She reached in and retrieved one of the tiniest bags. I took it from her.

"Is that all?" she asked.

"For now." I might have to return if I used up this ichor before I could locate the memories and information I needed. I turned away from the cooler and the dirty vendor and popped the cap of the tube on the ichor bag.

Most people try not drink ichor straight to dilute the taste. I don't usually mind how it tastes, which differs by the aeon from whom it flows. I put the tube to my lips and drained the bag with a single long pull.

At that moment, my senses heightened and the light gleamed even more bright and sickly. The smells of perfume and the sounds of bartering ran amplified through my mind. Ichor usually does that to people when taken fast. Trained sensocyclers can control this rush of senses and keep the enhanced perception for as long as a memeotect like me can maintain network access. My senses quickly dulled some but still remained sharper than normal.

I paced to a bench, perhaps leftover from the stadium's past, and sat down. I checked to see if the security officer working the ichor stand was in view and found him close enough to put my mind at ease a little. But still, if I dove into the network for any stretch of time the chance of getting my card stolen went up dramatically. I left the market, walked along the canal to the ferry and boarded. Nobody but the captain would even be watching.

I stood on the deck, near the center of the ship, and looked out at the sunlit canal waters. I took a deep breath, and then set my mind to sail through the network with a mental push.

The network appears to the mind's eye as a variety of things, but most of us notice how bright it seems. The threads of my consciousness unwound, spreading out through the mindscape like skinny tree branches. The minds of others connected to the network drifted around me at a distance. I was at once both aware of them and uninterested. I sent my thoughts through the market where not many were using. Cleans never used ichor so they were invisible to the light network approach I had at the moment. With enough ichor in my system, I could detect the minds of anyone in the region.

I worked through the minds of these people slowly, searching for any facts that would prove to me that the woman was Rebecca.

Rebecca, with her laughter, head thrown back, and shawl tossed to the ground. Rebecca with her ambition to go east from the Green Valley where the two of us had grown up. Rebecca who gave me hope when I was a geeky kid who always finished behind his older brother.

I sighed at the thoughts but kept looking. The network helped me ignore the cold of the day, but it wasn't until I turned my thoughts to the memories I kept within me that I lost all perception of the outside world.

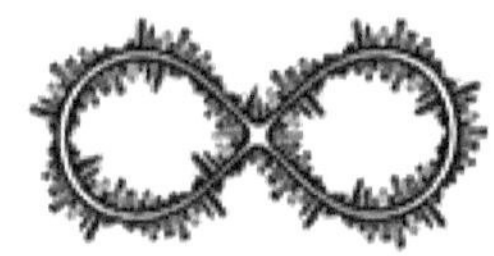

UNREGISTERED MEMORY, Spring 2063

In the Green Valley in the center of the wildlands between the great cities of the east coast and west coast spring brought rain that swelled the river and turned the dirt of country roads into mud. I lived in a town a few hours from nowhere. There was one aeon in the whole county where I grew up, a member of the first generation named Kedhos. I never met him, but like everyone, I had a daily relationship with his blood, his ichor.

I was walking a forested path, trying to not get my sneakers too filthy with the mud that sucked at them with every step. To avoid the worst of the mud, I walked along the side where the leaves provided a thin covering for the pitch-black mixture of dirt and water. Birds chirped in the trees, sometimes startling me.

I had a messenger bag tucked under one arm. I'd had that bag for years, and at thirteen, there wasn't a lot more important to me in the world than its contents, a worn blue folder containing photographs of people and places from before the rise of the aeons. I had brought it with me that day to see if I could find some of the landmarks it mentioned from the city closest to my hometown.

As I walked, I considered how it was too bad that aeons had needed to tear apart the world I saw in those images. Once, there had been cities in and around the Green Valley, but now they were dust, swept under the roots of tall trees.

Those trees and their stubborn frost-resistant leaves gave the valley its new name. I picked up my feet and pressed forward to climb a trail of mud up the hillside to a place where the path met a paved highway. The road's asphalt surface was pocked with craters and split with cracks, but it wasn't muddy, and it pointed the way back to town.

I walked along the road for a mile before the town came into view, spread over a slope that formed one of the earliest foothills of the valley's edge. Once, my brother and I climbed to the top of the tower that stood on the hill's peak and looked east to see the route the trains still used to get between the coasts, cutting across plains of waving grass.

But on that road, thoughts of the world outside the valley felt fanciful. I followed the curve of the road toward town and was less than a half mile from my house, near the western edge where the ground softened and we risked flooding every year in the spring, when the sound of a loud combustion engine made me turn to look back.

A single vehicle appeared around the bend of the road, a white van with dirty sides and a cracked windshield. I watched the van approach with its roaring engine and the smell of fuel drifting closer. The vehicle sputtered and slowed as it neared where I stood with my messenger bag tucked under one arm.

I raised my other arm and waved, as innocent as youth can be, never having seen a vehicle on this highway before. The van slowed and stopped not far from me. I walked toward it, searching through the windshield for whoever might be driving the old-fashioned machine.

A sliding door opened to the side where I couldn't see. Then the driver's door swung outward with a *clank*. I froze. A towering man with tanned skin and a thick black beard stepped out. A girl in a white and blue shawl that covered her hair came around the side from the sliding door. She looked to be about my age, skin the same color as the man's.

Her face came back to me in a rush, how Rebecca had looked when I'd first seen her. She was thinner and less healthy looking at thirteen, but her eyes were as beautiful as always. She smiled when she looked at me on the road.

"Father," she said. "It's a boy!"

The man with the fierce beard looked at me with a level gaze. "Are you from this area?" he asked.

I looked between the father and the girl with the entrancing eyes. "Y-Yes, yes," I said. "I'm from the town up there." I pointed at the hill where houses were interspersed among the trees. I looked at the father. "Are you travelers?"

"We're from further north." His dark eyes looked nothing like his daughter's. "But we're not travelers. We're settlers."

My eyes widened. I stammered out some words even the enhancements of ichor did not allow me to recall.

The father laughed. "Come on boy. Don't just stand there, I want you to show my family and me to town."

"It's right on the hillside," I said. "You probably don't need my help. Not really."

The girl walked up to me, and put her face close to mine. Her expression changed from playful amusement to gentle concern. "Father gets what he wants," she said softly. "Or he hurts people."

I swallowed and fell back a step from the girl. "Oh. Okay."

She led me to the van where a woman in a dark shawl held a young boy in her lap in a seat behind the driver. The girl and I sat beside them. She smiled weakly at me, then leaned close to my ear. "I'm sorry. But don't worry, I'll make sure he doesn't hurt you."

"Thanks," I said, suddenly very aware of this beautiful girl so close to me. "I won't forget."

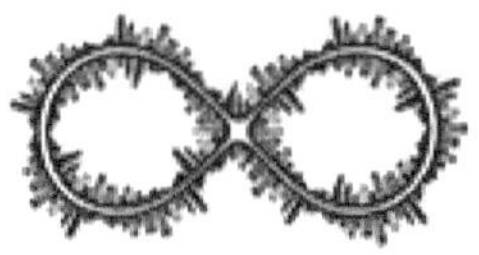

MY HEIGHTENED MEMORIES diminished as the ichor went inert in my system. By then dusk crept over the megalopolis from the seaside to the westernmost Aeon Heights. I shivered, my mind made up. I walked back to the market. Confidence drained from my mind like fading ichor with every step as I entered through the front gate. The lights inside the market were brighter than ever, casting my shadow across the ground.

Did I really dare do this? Elizabeth could still be sensitive even after we decided to limit our relationship to the professional, and I had almost no proof beyond the memories in my mind that this clean was

Rebecca. *Had been* Rebecca. Unless the whispered rumors of a cure for cleans were true.

Still, I walked to the stalls near where she had been dancing that morning. The giant still stood there, propped against an adjacent stall's side by one huge arm and still standing easily over two meters tall. His eyes moved toward me as I approached, but I ignored him.

I ducked the giant's tattooed arm and approached the raised area where this woman who so-resembled the Rebecca of my memories once again danced among the other cleans on display. Her form shifted, and she turned her face to scan the crowd. No expression graced her features beyond the simple bliss of emptiness that came with being cleaned.

I stared at her, eyes searching that face for a spark of recognition. One thing was certain—despite the gulf of time and place—she was Rebecca.

I stifled my cry of dismay with one hand to my mouth. Then a man's heavy arm fell around my shoulders. It was the giant. "Sir," he said. "I take it you see something on display you like?"

My eyes moved to meet the grinning face of the huge man. I stammered, "I-I believe I might."

"You know the dancers on display are among the finest cleans sold at this market, especially on a day like today."

"I am aware. Are you selling?"

"Not all of them are mine." He whistled and pointed at the clean that looked like Rebecca. *It can't be her,* I told myself. *It must not be her. She must be free, probably having long forgotten me, but free.* "That one is. She goes by the name of Rain."

"Rain?" I said.

"That's her name."

I looked at Rain's face, unsure of myself with the giant's arm still across my shoulders. "I am sorry," I said. "How much for Re-For Rain?"

"You make up your mind fast, my friend. Don't you want to know where this one comes from first?"

"Let me guess," I said.

He shook his head. "You'll never figure it out."

"Have you ever heard of a place called the Green Valley?" I asked.

His jaw dropped ever so slightly, betraying his surprise. "Someone you knew?"

"No," I lied, "but I happen to have an eye for the middle country."

"You must, but there aren't many of her kind out there."

"And what kind is that?"

"No need to get testy, sir."

"Fine. How much for her?"

He released my shoulder and looked me up and down. "Two thousand."

Two thousand. That would have made up a sizable portion of my investment in the network building I was planning on renting with Elizabeth soon. Of course, we didn't strictly need a building being that we could relay everything by ourselves using ichor in our own apartments, but it could help for when we had more staff, and Elizabeth wanted more staff. But I made over two thousand in a month when I was working on high commission for the Aeon Omasoa's network as I had been doing lately.

I stared at this woman called Rain, whose mind had been cleaned by the aeons. I closed my eyes for a moment, frowning. Thomas would be curious. He would ask about her. I knew right away I would tell him the truth. For all his baseness at times, Thomas was a good friend. Rain's eyes opened, at last, sparkling and dark. Those eyes, that face. These belonged to Rebecca, whatever she had become.

"I'll take her." I held out my cred card to the giant man. *Now that face, those eyes will belong to me.*

The giant took the card and scanned it. "A pleasure doing business with you, sir. Just give us a moment to get her down and dressed."

"Thank you," I said.

And I meant it. I'd never missed anyone like I missed Rebecca. Cleaned or not, I wanted to be near her again. And I couldn't bear to see her taken away by some slave master or brothel owner. Part of me warred with these thoughts because that part of me knew, even if she resembled Rebecca, *Rain* did not know me. Rain did not care if she spent her remaining days in some brothel being sold to anyone who could afford her for an hour, a night, a day.

The giant sent a more ordinary-looking man up to the platform to retrieve Rain. When the man returned with her she wore a long coat of shabby gray material. "Is this acceptable?" the giant asked me.

"I think so," I said.

The giant leered at Rain. "You think?"

"It's fine."

"Stars be with you friend." The giant turned to the other man who pushed Rain gently from the back, directing her toward me. "If you have any trouble with her, here is my card. I'll gladly take her off your hands, at least until the market closes next month."

"Thanks." I took the man's card as well as my cred card. I wanted to scream at myself. What was I doing? She's clean. The Rebecca I knew is dead. Yes, but if there's even a chance... A chance of what?

Everyone knows the cleans cannot be restored, only urban legends say otherwise. I stuffed the card in my pants pocket and took Rain's soft hand as gently as I could. "Hello, Rain," I said softly.

"Hello."

"Jethro," I said. "Call me Jeth."

"Jeth?" Her voice reached my ears, so familiar. Her breath touched my neck as she passed close to me.

"Yeah," I said. Some structure inside of me collapsed at the questioning tone of her voice. She really remembered nothing.

I took Rain's hand and led her away from her former owners. When we reached the center of the path, I stopped and looked around for

Thomas. My friend was walking toward me, leading a handful of cleans and checking his card's light cell to see how much he could still afford on it.

"Well, well." He looked at Rain, then at me. "Mister Jethro Gall, it looks like something could tempt you after all."

"Someone," I said. Then I leaned closer to him, one hand still holding onto Rain. "I'll tell you the rest later."

He raised an eyebrow. "Alright," he said. "I don't get it, but alright."

"Maybe I should go back to the ferry."

I stared at Thomas, brows bent, and hoped he got my meaning.

He nodded. "Sure, Jeth. I think we've got everything you need right now." He clapped me on the shoulder, almost jarring my grip on Rain's hand loose. But I didn't let go. I turned and led Rain out of the old stadium that now served as a trading ground for empty-minded cleans.

2

THAT EVENING, RAIN and I rode the ferry back to Lotdel Tower district, sharing the vessel with Thomas and his dozen or so new additions to the Mangrove Suite. I decided we should stay on deck despite the falling temperatures because I didn't want to lose track of Rain among the other cleans.

The night sky lit up with ghostly aeon lights that danced from the skyline. I stood by the tower of the bridge, watching the heart of the city grow closer. Rain shivered beside me, and I resisted the urge to put my arm around her. It would do me no good to think of a clean as a person. Though, if that was the case why had I bought her?

She pressed herself to my side, seeking warmth. Her touch thrilled me, as much as it would were she still Rebecca. I wrapped an arm around her shoulders. "Should we go inside?" I asked.

"Is it warm inside?"

I frowned, taken aback by the clean's lucidity. I had never really tried to communicate with a clean before, not as an adult at least, but I did not expect such a human answer in a perfectly normal voice.

"Yes," I said.

She stared at me wide-eyed. "Please. Let's go in."

"Alright." I led her toward the entrance, guiding her with my arm.

When we entered the ferry's upper hallway, I found Thomas waiting by the door, back leaned against the wall.

"Jeth," he said.

"Thomas."

"I think it's time you came clean," he said. "Just this morning you told me you weren't going to buy anything."

"Anyone."

"Forget your damn terms for a minute, Jeth!" Thomas pushed his back off the wall and faced me. "You bought a girl."

I swallowed bile. "I recognized her."

"You what?" He put a hand to his ear.

"Recognized her." I glowered at Thomas. "She's an old friend."

"She's a clean. Cleans aren't friends with anyone." Thomas folded his arms. His eyes moved to Rain, who was still pressed to my side.

"I know what you're saying." I held back my anger at Thomas' words. What he said was common knowledge. Cleans don't remember anything. Cleans don't want anything but pleasure. "I just... I knew her when she was human."

He took in a sharp hiss of breath. "So, you bought her."

"Yeah, I bought her."

Thomas sighed. "You know how bad this idea is?"

"I didn't want to see her taken away. Again." I clenched the fist at my side. "I didn't think about the consequences."

"You sure as hell didn't. What's Elizabeth going to say?"

"I don't know, but I can guess she won't be happy."

He shook his head. "Look, I want to help you. Maybe she could stay at the Mangrove Suite while you explain things to Elizabeth."

"I'd be alright with that if you promise me one thing."

"She won't work any clients. Cross my heart and drown me if I should lie."

I looked up at him. He appeared earnest. I unclenched my fist. "Thanks."

"It's nothing. You still have to tell Elizabeth about her."

"Do I? Me and Elizabeth, we're just business partners."

"She may be under a different impression, Jeth. I shouldn't have to tell you that."

I felt heat in my face. "I'm not leading her on."

"I know. Okay. Let's focus. What are we going to do about her?"

I released my hold on Rain's shoulder. She stepped to one side of me and Thomas, looking at the space between us with an empty gaze.

"I don't know," I said, "but haven't you heard the stories? The stories of cleans being restored by aeons."

He frowned. "I've heard stories, Jeth, but I don't think the cleans want it. They gave up their humanity to escape from pain, not because they were forced into it."

"You're right." But was he? I couldn't believe Rebecca would willingly give up her mind. "Forget I mentioned it."

"No problem. I really wish you hadn't brought that up in the first place." He frowned. "Look, Jeth. I think we'll have to see what happens. I'll take her with me tonight. She can stay in the Mangrove Suite until you and I decide what to do."

"Okay."

"I need to check on the other cleans."

I nodded.

Thomas turned and walked down a passage to the cabins. I turned to Rain.

"Warm," she said.

"Yeah." I smiled at her.

She gave me an expressionless gaze in return.

We reached shore and took Thomas' aging gray van to Lotdel Tower. There, Rain and I parted. Thomas took her up to the fortieth floor of the gleaming skyscraper that was Lotdel Tower. I rode the elevator to the twelfth floor, where my apartment overlooked Bailey Court Garden and its always-green central trees.

I drew the curtains and sat down on my bed. Tomorrow, I'd be back to work at my network, and I'd be back to making plans with Elizabeth, but tonight, I needed to remember why I missed Rebecca so much. I needed to remember because a wall had come tumbling down today, a barrier I didn't ever expect to fall.

I lay back on the bed, darkness and warmth all around, and I closed my eyes.

UNREGISTERED MEMORY, 2066

When I was sixteen and living as a student in the Green Valley far to the west, I had one great friend. Her name was Rebecca Malik, and I loved her.

The two of us went through life like any other students at the time, almost fifty years after the rise of the aeons. We shared a few classes, physics and biology, and we sat side by side during them. Neither of us paid much attention to the material.

I was more interested in memeotecture and the advanced study of ideas relayed by ichor. Without reliable electronics because of the war, the biological-ichor relay had become indisputably the best way for humans to communicate over great distances to mass audiences. Rebecca loved memeotecture even more than I did. She took to constructing thoughts for others from her own mind easily.

Rebecca and I drank our ichor cups in the morning like the nectar of the gods. Some people still think of aeons as gods so I suppose that makes sense. They sure seemed like it at the time. Ichor enhances human senses and gives us access to sensory and memetic networks.

Her parents were hard on her. And they never liked me or ichor much. Some days she would come to school with bruises. On those days, she wouldn't say a word to anyone but me and wouldn't answer when called on in class. She told me it was her father, trying to beat the evil out of her.

I told her she shouldn't take that kind of thing from anyone.

Through all of it, I thought we'd grown closer than she must have. Because she left for the east coast five years before I did. A week after her sixteenth birthday, she jumped a train and rode out of my life. She left me a note at school, delivered by our dull-eyed homeroom teacher. The last line is the only part I remembered clearly.

I'm sorry I won't see you again, Jeth, but you would do the same if you were in my shoes.

I was angry for a long time.

Eventually, the anger faded. Then I just missed her.

Five years after she left, I followed the railway as far as I could go on foot, the side of the great highway leading out of the Green Valley and across the hills. I hitched a ride on a truck that burned diesel like an athlete burns calories. That truck carried me to the east.

I never forgot Rebecca, but I thought I'd never see her again.

When I woke in the morning, the day after buying Rain, I still wasn't sure if I would or not.

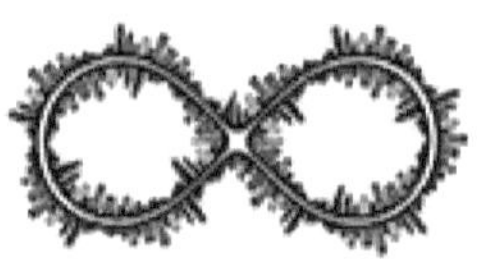

I LEFT MY APARTMENT for the restaurant on the tenth floor around seven in the morning. Nageddia, the aeon who owned Lotdel Tower, mandated a credit-free breakfast for all inhabitants of the building. Apparently, she didn't like to see people underfed. I brought the smaller of my two ichor flasks with me, because I had to work today, and met Elizabeth when I stepped out the elevator doors.

The doors closed behind me.

Elizabeth smiled from under waves of golden brown hair. "Good morning," she said. "Guess Thomas didn't keep you out too late."

I blinked at her. "I suppose he didn't." I smiled with all the weariness I felt. "The real issue is the travel time, you know."

"Why'd you want to see a clean market anyway?"

"I'm not really sure. I guess part of me is fascinated by them. The cleans, I mean."

"I knew what you meant." We walked to the doorway leading to the open restaurant. "I guess it's all the ichor, isn't it?"

I frowned. Even though I refused to use ichor except on work days I did sometimes overdo it for shaping scenes and thoughts.

"You may be right. I suppose you've also heard that many of them were previously insane from ichor overdose."

"That's a rumor. I've never actually seen an aeon clean someone."

I frowned as we walked to a table in an alcove of the ornately gilded square room. She set her purse in one seat, and we headed for the sparse line. They served all sorts of food that would be familiar to people across the country. Fried and scrambled eggs in a tub beside bacon, and on the other side, a large coffee machine dispensed hot water and fragrant mix. Fresh fruit sat along the opposite side of the food line.

"You don't have to see it to know it happens," she said. "Jeth, are you in a bad mood?"

"What do you mean?"

She shrugged. "I don't think it's worth arguing before we have something to eat."

She dished up some eggs, then turned to a salad bowl.

I put a few strips of bacon on my plate, then headed straight for the fresh fruit. A lot of guys my size tried to steer clear of eggs when possible, but I never did. I backed up and took some of those, too. If I was trying to eat healthily, I would have cut out the bacon, but I liked bacon the most. I took an apple and a few strawberries. Then, I turned to face Elizabeth.

"You don't honestly think I'm trying to argue, do you?"

"You seem pretty riled."

I shrugged. "I guess I had a rough night."

"Tell me about it," she said and headed for the table in the alcove.

I followed her, still reluctant to tell her the truth about Rain. But I knew I'd need to do it sometime. If Thomas could be trusted with this, Elizabeth definitely could. We sat down across from each other. She looked down at her plate, apparently thinking. Then she picked up her purse and removed a small purple plastic bottle that contained her daily ichor.

She poured it into the cup at her seat. A lot of memeotects wake up without coffee. The amount of ichor it takes to activate a network is always relatively large compared to simply attaining enhanced senses so the heightening of energy is significant as well. It's like caffeine, but with less crash and more addictiveness.

Elizabeth sipped her ichor. "You ready to tell me what happened?"

I frowned. "It's the clean market," I said, then paused, chewing on my thoughts. "I saw someone familiar there."

"Familiar? Jeth, the megalopolis has a population of at least a hundred million people, but the market isn't that far down the canal from here."

"It wasn't someone I knew from the megalopolis," I said. "She was a girl I knew back in the Green Valley."

"You knew her..."

"Liz, it was never like that." A stretch maybe, but I didn't want to get into that with Elizabeth. "We were friends."

"Now she's here, though."

"Well, not exactly." I couldn't believe I was doing this, but the words kept spilling out. "Liz, she's been cleaned."

Elizabeth's eyes widened slightly. Everyone knows the cleans used to be people, but nobody likes to think of friends or family going that way and losing their minds. My partner, strictly my business partner, cleared her throat.

"Jeth, I'm sorry."

I clenched my flask in my hand. "Don't be sorry," I said. "It's not your fault."

She reached out and put a hand on mine, easing the flask back toward the table. "Jeth, I'm glad you told me."

I shook my head. "That's not all, Liz."

She frowned.

I looked up from her hand on the hand that held the flask. "I bought her."

Elizabeth's hand withdrew from mine. The color rushed to her face. "You bought her?"

I nodded.

Elizabeth's lip trembled. She sniffed in a breath and sat back in her chair. Her gaze moved to the cup of ichor on the table between us. "I guess that explains it," she said.

"Explains what?"

"Why you don't want to talk to me today. You slept with her, didn't you?"

"No, nothing like that!" My face heated up, and I scowled. "I did not sleep with her."

"You didn't?" She crossed her arms. "You expect me to believe that?"

"It's the truth! She stayed in the Mangrove Suite last night. Thomas took her there."

She flushed despite her scowl. "You may want to rethink that phrasing."

I shook my head, fire coursing in my blood. I raised the flask of ichor to my lips, then hesitated. "I thought you were grateful I told you. I couldn't lie, you know."

She nodded but didn't look at all mollified. "Fine." She drained her cup of ichor.

I downed the contents of my flask. The energy of the ichor flowed into me, and my senses heightened. I reached out with my mind, feeling the mental presence of Elizabeth and the cooks and waiters. My feelings expanded, giving me the sense of filling up the room, then the building, then the city.

I reached into my mind, knowing my eyes were glazing over visibly, but also knowing Elizabeth was doing the same because of the aura that built around her mind, heavily woven and beautifully intricate.

Every mind has a different sense to it, different aptitudes and weaknesses, and they present as different forms and senses in the mental world.

I set my hands on the table and felt the hardwood beneath my palms. It pulsed with the mantle of the earth far below the surface, but here it almost made the polished tree remains feel alive again. More alive than ever because now they seemed to be breathing. The feeling of new life was normal, but every time it took a few minutes to recede.

My mind's willowy expanse brushed against the finely crafted fortress of Elizabeth's. She blinked and her eyes returned to normal. I tried to normalize as fast as I could, but in the meantime, I built an image of the clean market and sent it to Elizabeth through the network we formed locally through our proximity to each other.

I chose the images that showed the bizarre objectification of the cleans, the dancers, the sellers in their perfume-laden stalls.

Then I normalized with a hiccup. "Sorry," I said, "but I couldn't leave her like that."

Elizabeth nodded. "I don't really understand, but I'm glad you didn't try to keep her secret."

I put a fist to my chest and took a deep breath, trying to still the incessant hiccups that threatened to disrupt my entire mentality. Finally, the sensation of unrest in my diaphragm faded. "I appreciate it. I wouldn't lie to you, partner."

She nodded again, but her smile from earlier was long gone.

3

THE MENTAL ALARM NORMALLY embedded deep in my subconscious went off about five minutes after Elizabeth and I finished breakfast and were on our way out of the restaurant. It did not blare harsh sounds but spoke in the gentle voice of Nageddia, the aeon owner of Lotdel Tower. She lived near the tower. and it was her responsibility to inform the tenants.

"A rogue star has been sighted in the local district. Please use caution when leaving your buildings."

Elizabeth glanced at me and mouthed, "A rogue star?"

I shook my head. "I dunno." Rogue stars could be any sort of inhuman monster from beyond the city, outside of any aeon's control. When they infiltrated, they could kill a lot of people who got too close unless the aeons stopped them first.

The message repeated a few more times, but then fell silent. Elizabeth and I headed for the elevator down to the first floor. "You think it's actually dangerous?" I asked.

She shrugged. "I doubt it. There are thousands of aeons in the megalopolis, not to mention all the purifiers and the Teloite guards."

I nodded, but I didn't like the names she brought up. Purifiers were human but invested with the right to act as police and inquisition in the megalopolis. The Teloites were even worse as far as I was concerned, a gang of extremists, both human and aeon, acting as extra-jurisdictional law enforcement. Aeons used their own ichor to boost their physical strength and vitality so they could be a match for most rogue stars.

My ichor let me connect to networks for news, so I did as the elevator moved down to the first floor. The voice of the Grand

Network's newscaster, Peter Harrison, echoed in my mind. "The rogue star sighted in the Central Megalopolis is likely some kind of creature composed by the beast forces across the sea. It may have physical powers at its command. Do not approach any unusual individuals. The rogue star is reportedly capable of creating very convincing disguises." Peter had a harsh voice for delivery in general, and today was worse than normal. Each word sounded as though it had to be scraped off the roof of his mouth. His company evidently wouldn't let him change it or mask it with emotions or other feelings, even though that would be simple over the network.

Things always seem worse after a big change, I reminded myself. *And yesterday, I found Rebecca.* If that wasn't a big change I didn't know what was. Elizabeth glanced at me. "Are you okay?" she said. "The network news doesn't seem all that bad."

"I need to go into work today," I said. It was true, but more than anything I wanted to be able to say the opposite. "Omasoa wants to see how productive we can be."

"She'll understand if you're late. Aeons aren't monsters."

Funny saying, that. "I know what you mean," I said, "but this is important."

We stepped into the elevator. Elizabeth hit the controls for the first floor before I could do anything. I glanced at her. She smiled at me. "You could use a head start. If anyone does, you need the help today."

Normally, I thought Elizabeth would make a great newscaster or network branch. She really did have a way with words sometimes. Too bad this wasn't one of them.

"Thanks," I said. The elevator doors closed in front of us, and we rode down to the first-floor entrance.

I stepped out of the elevator, and Elizabeth took it back up. I made my way to the front doors. They stood open, and I shivered at the breeze blowing through them. As I approached the doors, I found myself looking out into a cloud-covered city, as if bulging gray curtains moved through the air above the earth.

Wind blustered through the streets, carrying the first drops of a rainstorm. I pulled my coat around me and headed out into it. My every other thought turned back to Rebecca, still in the Mangrove Suite. I would have liked to see her again and talk to Thomas before I went to work, but I didn't want to do anything else to make Elizabeth angry with me.

I walked across the street o the train station. I was late for the first train of the day and twenty minutes shy of the second. The warning on the network had rattled me a bit. A rogue star of all things. Star was another way people sometimes referred to aeons, but a rogue could hardly be anything but one turned into a beast and crossing the wasteland or the sea. I did not dare activate my network connection to surf through information because of the warning.

Silly, I thought, as I waited on the bench at the train station lit by veins of glowing blue that crept across the concrete ceiling. *It's not as though a rogue star would be looking for me.* I tried to relax as I picked up a newspaper from the stand and paid with my cred card. The print news aggregated plenty of information left untouched or buried in the mind networks. With computers remaining highly disliked by aeons in general, and considered less than reliable with any aeon around, I suppose people saw the wisdom in reverting to the older form of distribution.

My fingers turned the pages absently. I skipped over a section of local obituaries to read the news of the war in the west. Beasts preyed on the opposite coast's megalopolis far more than they ever approached us here in the east. In general, I was glad for it, but I couldn't help but look it up. My older brother, Luke, had moved out west just a few weeks before I followed Rebecca east. He'd gone to become a journalist, and he'd had stories published across the country by both memeotects over the network and print papers.

The train whistle blew as it pulled into the station. I rose from the bench, folding my paper as I went. As I approached the train to board, a voice came from behind me. Ryan Carter. "Jeth, wait up!"

I turned as skinny little Ryan sprinted across the terminal. His bag banged into his side with every step. He stopped before me, breathing hard. He looked at me with a grin. Then together we boarded the train.

"Morning," I said.

"Pretty good, yeah," he said. "You hear about the rogue star?"

"How could I miss it?" I said. "I suppose that's why you're working at the office today?" Ryan was a defensive analyst at a technical combat company near where I worked in the area north of Lotdel Tower.

He nodded vigorously. "Yep, gotta protect the city and all that."

I shook my head. "What would you do if you ran into a rogue star yourself?"

"Call for backup," he said without hesitation. "I'm an analyst, not a soldier."

I grinned. "Good attitude. I wouldn't want to face down one of those monsters either."

The train started moving as we found seats. It was sparsely packed. Not many people who had jobs in knowledge went to work every day because of the network and most of the time they wouldn't want to if they knew a rogue star was roaming the neighborhood. Hopefully, the train would take us clear of danger zone. Where there were more aeons, things would surely be safer.

I leaned back in my seat and opened the newspaper.

"Anything good in there?" Ryan asked.

"Not in particular," I said, going back to my search for any news on the western war. I found what I was looking for a few seconds later, between an article on a new generator heart maturing out at the Aeon Heights west of the more packed parts of the city and an ad for a network I didn't recognize.

"The western forces pushed elements of a beast unit back toward the interior."

"The war again?" Ryan said.

I glanced at him.

He shrugged. "You were reading about the war last time we ran into each other on the train."

"My brother's out there."

"But he's not a soldier. He'll be fine, Jeth."

"I guess I'm not so sure about that. Luke once went to poke a hornet's nest. Literally. And he didn't even use a stick."

Ryan laughed. "Bet that gave him some interesting lumps."

I smirked. "You have no idea. But my point is, Luke doesn't have a lot of common sense."

"I get what you mean."

"Well then." I shook my head. "You can see how I might think he'd go diving into danger when he really doesn't have any need."

Ryan nodded, still smiling from his burst of laughter. "Really, a hornet's nest? You gotta be kidding me."

"I wish."

"Your brother wishes."

"Well, I was right next to him."

Ryan's palm flew to his forehead. "Somebody should have put a leash on you two!"

I shrugged. Rebecca had told me I'd be better off not following Luke around after that. "That was Green Valley life," I said.

"I bet." Ryan spoke between wheezes of mirth. "Do any of you middlers think before you act?"

"Not in general." I thought of Rain who had once been Rebecca, sitting in a sweetly perfumed room in the Mangrove Suite. That was one piece of information I wouldn't be sharing with Ryan or anyone beside Thomas and Elizabeth, if I had my way.

The train lurched at its next stop. The doors on either side of our car slid open. Through one of them, a bearded man in a button-down shirt and blue jeans stepped. He shook his head fitfully, possibly from an over-consumption of ichor. Sometimes people went overboard, and if one did that too much, one could end up cleaned. Like Rebecca. The more I thought about her, the more I considered the possibility that things could have happened exactly that way.

My fingers tightened together, tearing the sides of the newspaper where I gripped it.

"Woah, Jeth, what's the matter?" Ryan asked.

"Nothing," I said. "Just thought I might lose my grip."

He shrugged his shoulders. "If you say so."

The doors slid shut, and the train started moving again. I watched the man who'd just entered, more and more sure he had overdosed on ichor. He rubbed his palms against each other, then pressed them both to his forehead. His eyes quickly turned glassy from network access. He stood like that for a minute or two, stock still, hands pressed to his forehead.

Then he let out a gasp of air and collapsed to the floor of the train car.

Ryan was out of his seat in one instant and by the man's side in another. He checked the man's pulse immediately, a trained first responder. I rose more slowly and looked around the train car. "Is anyone here a doctor?"

None of the other half a dozen passengers answered except with looks of nervousness in their eyes.

I knelt beside Ryan and the fallen man, who I then saw was breathing. "He's not dying?" I said. The ichor overdosed man on the floor of the train could be a threat to all of us on board if he turned into a beast.

"He's already mad, most likely," said Ryan, "but the ichor he overdosed on will turn him into a beast if we don't move quickly."

"I understand." I accessed my network even as I spoke. My mind reached through space and time, and I signaled the universal distress call to the aeons. The nearest visible aeon mind gleamed in my mental sight, two dozen blocks across the city at our destination, Omasoa, and even she could not stop a train in motion. I cut the network connection. "This isn't good," I said. "How long do we have?"

"I don't know," said Ryan. "Do you think I'm an expert on beasts?"

I shook my head. The car sped across the city, rising from the ground on elevated tracks. I glanced around the car once again. "Damn it," I muttered. "If he turns before we come to the next stop, we'll be stuck on here with him."

Ryan nodded, eyes focused on the man on the floor.

I felt a gentle hand on my shoulder, a feminine touch, followed by a woman's low voice. "Remain calm."

The flicker of an image slipped through my mental barriers and evaded my antibodies. The image was of Rebecca, wearing a business suit. She turned to face my vantage point, but then the vision faded.

The woman on the train passed me and Ryan, a long black coat flowing around her shoulders. She knelt beside the man on the floor, softly moving Ryan away from him. Her hair was shockingly pale, nearly white, and I couldn't see her face because of its length and thickness.

She placed one small hand on the man's forehead, and in that moment, I glimpsed a trickle of pale gold flowing from her palm. *Ichor.* The strange woman, who I had somehow, impossibly, not noticed before the moment she touched my shoulder, eased the wound flowing with ichor over the man's eyes. Her body tensed for a moment. Then she withdrew her hand.

The man opened his eyes, seeing clearly, but I knew nothing mattered to him anymore.

This impossible woman was an aeon. And she had just cleaned this man.

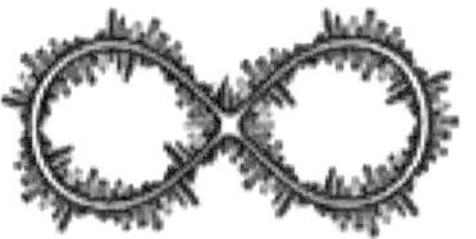

4

THE WOMAN STRAIGHTENED her back and raised the hood of a sweatshirt under her coat. She turned without me seeing her face and strode past me. Her long sleeves hid the aeon wounds in her palms. Normally, one cannot see into the mind of an aeon without their intent. For some reason, she had showed me an image of Rebecca. This aeon had known her. My focus fixed on the end of her sleeve.

Each aeon has five wounds. No more. No less. From each wound flows ichor. Every child learned these things in school.

I had never seen an aeon clean someone before, but the vacant joy on the man's face struck me as obvious. He was clean. Ryan spoke to him, but the man shook his head. He stared adoringly after the woman who had just wiped his mind away. I gritted my teeth. She may have saved me, but I hated to see it. I hated to think of someone doing the same thing to Rebecca.

The woman paused at my side, long coat flowing to the floor. "Why are you angry, Jethro?" I glanced up at her, still unable to see her face through the strands of white-blonde hair and the dark hood. She bowed her head slightly and full lips curved, the only visible part of her face.

I sat hunched, paralyzed. Everything had happened so suddenly. She took another step as if to move on. I had not detected her. How could that have been?

In defiance of good sense, my hand snaked out and I seized her forearm before she could pass me by. "Wait!"

She did not struggle or resist my touch on her sleeve. She shook her head. "Jethro, be calm."

"You saved the life of every person in this car." I raised my voice as I continued. "Please, tell us your name."

"My name," she said, "Is Yashelia. Please, unhand me, human."

I did not relax my grip. The other people in the car stared at the two of us, locked together by my hand. She looked down at me, at last. I grimaced. "How do you know my name?"

"You assume we aeons would require means you would understand to learn of you."

"I've never heard of an aeon called Yashelia," I said.

"Then you are poorly informed."

"Oh, am I?" I looked forward. Ryan turned toward me. He shook his head as if to tell me to stop my press on this woman. She would have appeared on the network when I had sent the warning to the aeons.

This is the rogue star.

"So, you figured it out?" she said.

And she can hear my thoughts, regardless of my safeguards.

I put all my strength into hauling her down. She struggled then, but not for long. Ichor suffuses the body of every aeon and, unlike humans, they are built for exploiting it to gain improved strength and speed. She moved herself like a whip, and I hit the ceiling with a *crunch*. My back screamed in protest. My mind flooded with pain. I had only a moment to hesitate before I fell to the floor of the car. Again, pain exploded through my hands and knees. Shock ran through both arms. I groaned.

Whatever she was as a rogue star, she worked a lot like an aeon. Yashelia spun to face me. Her hood fell back, revealing a beautiful face, but one pale as death. Ryan stumbled to his feet. He backed away from Yashelia, not making even a small move to help me. I didn't blame him.

Her flawless nose wrinkled. "I take it you know what a rogue star would do in this situation?"

I glared up at her from my hands and knees. "You plan to kill all of us. Monster."

She smirked, then turned and walked past me to the sliding door. One of my arms gave out under me, and I fell, feeling sticky blood run down my arm inside my sleeve and coating my skinned hands. Yashelia ignored me. She pried the door open with her fingers, tearing metal and breaking locks. Cold air rushed in from the autumn of the city. Yashelia glanced back at me. "Until we meet again," she said in a booming voice that drowned the rushing of the air, "Jethro."

Yashelia threw herself from the train car. She caught like a mote of dust in the air and glided over the low rooftops and out of sight. I stared after her from my place on the ground, unable to move except to roll onto my side.

Ryan ran to my side. "Jeth, are you alright?"

I grunted and nodded, but I never took my eyes off the open door on the side of the train car. The light veins above us shimmered as the train continued to drive north. Ryan helped me sit up, and I ached all over. My back protested most movement so I sat on the floor of the car for the rest of the trip to our stop.

MY SPINE WAS INTACT, and both arms were swiftly repaired by the heartlink I attached to them when I arrived at the office. Ryan had helped me get there once we reached the station, before heading on to his own office at security. The aeon who managed my network, Omasoa, came down to meet me while I sat with aching, if whole, limbs in the break room on the fifteenth floor of our forty-story office complex.

She wore her hair long like most aeons, and the dark locks framed her face. She was a typical aeon in a lot of ways, I supposed, beautiful to the eye, and careful to wear no covering on her hands so her wounds were prominent, two fine holes drilled one through each palm.

I did my best to cover the surprise on my face as I bowed to her when she entered the room. "Ma'am."

She walked to the break room table, followed by her assistant. "Jethro Gall," she said in a voice higher than Yashelia's, familiar, more girlish. "I hear you had an interesting encounter on the train today. A rogue star is dangerous, and you are but a human. I do not want to lose your work for some foolish sense of duty you hold. Do not take that chance again."

I raised my head from my bow. "I understand."

"Good," she said. "With that in mind, take today easy."

"Ma'am, I can work."

"And I expect you to, but do not push your tolerance for either ichor or physical action any more than you already have."

I nodded. "I will be as responsible as I can be."

"Good." Omasoa turned and left the room. Her secretary followed behind her. I rarely spoke to any aeon as much as I had spoken to Omasoa over the past few minutes. They were usually so aloof from humans I had been surprised to even see Omasoa come to speak with me. Most of the time, when people got injured, the aeons sent a representative. Aeons almost never spoke to those affected for themselves.

"Huh," I said and sat back in my chair. I activated my network absently. From here, I had proximity to the storehouses of memetics that would allow me to work.

My job had me constructing information packets to be distributed by sensotects. I rarely transmitted much of the information personally because it required a lot of ichor, though all professional memeotects had to have a little understanding of sensocycles to do their jobs. I compiled the data and then sent it to a sensotect to distribute.

I searched through the raw data materials, as if rummaging around in drawers of infinite light and uncounted bits of information. Computer technology was too distrusted by aeons to store most of the material we used. Mostly, it was kept in the minds of people, lower journalists, who sought out new information constantly. Memeotects like me, and Elizabeth, and once Rebecca, would take the information and sort it, prepare it, and then convert it into packets understandable by the minds of other humans over sense networks. Casters like Peter Harrison would frame the information using their own voices and self-images to give things a human touch and a spin.

I worked as hard as anyone that day, but my mind was elsewhere, even more elsewhere than usual while diving through banks of information as deep as the Grand Canyon and twice as long. The locus of my private thoughts remained on the Mangrove Suite, and on Rain. Memeotects need to practice to hold back their thoughts, but it is quite possible to network without exposing everyone to your dreams and feelings.

Rain had looked so beautiful dancing, but her eyes were empty. Though I had rarely thought of it before, I knew there had to be some way to restore her mind. Aeons could clean humans who overdosed on ichor, and for all I knew, they would simply restore any mind they reset to a state of madness rather than its prior sanity. I went looking in the information piles on my lunch break, searching for facts related to clean restorations.

My efforts turned up nothing I didn't already know. And soon, I was back to work. By the time I was informed over the network that I could leave for home early, I was burning with the need to see her again, Rain, my angelic husk of a woman.

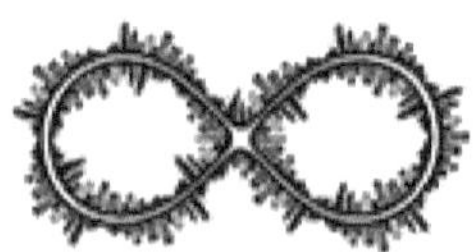

THE ELEVATOR CARRIED me up to the Mangrove Suite. I went there straight away, not wanting to run into Elizabeth before I could see Rebecca, or Rain as she now called herself. The machinery rumbled beneath me, then stilled. I stepped out of the elevator and into the warm, mute lights of the lobby of the Mangrove Suite.

Deep maroon carpet covered the floors. Soft laughter, that of a woman, lilted down the hallway that led to the rooms where the cleans were kept. Lived. Whatever. A wastebasket by the elevator looked as though it had never been used. I stood in front of the elevator for a moment with no other human in sight, unsure of what to do.

My skin crawled despite knowing Thomas ran the place as above board as he could. Some places just can't ever get all the way clean of evil. Still reluctant, I forced myself to walk down the hall toward the rooms and the woman's laughter. A desk and a guard stood in a semicircular room between the elevator and the rest of the suite.

The guard, another black man almost as large as me, and built a lot meaner, wearing a suit, crossed his arms. I didn't know him, so odds were I would need to ask for Thomas to get through. His face was impassive. "Do you have a reservation?"

"I'm not a customer," I said. "I'm a friend of Thomas Fenstein."

He raised an eyebrow. "You a friend of the boss."

"My name is Jethro Gall. He may have mentioned I'd be by today."

"You know, I don't think he mentioned you."

Keep cool. It won't do any good to get into a mix up with this guy. I met the man's eyes. He grinned. "There ain't no way I'm letting someone with such a weakass story through."

I clenched a fist. I may have been beaten by a rogue star earlier that day, but I wouldn't let that stop me from getting past Thomas' clueless flunky. "I'm telling the truth. Look!" I produced my wallet with City ID.

He shook his head, a shit-eating grin plastered to his face. "You know, this just keeps getting funnier and funnier. Get back on that elevator, you fuckin' bum." He laughed.

I glared at him. "Let me talk to Thomas."

"Oh, Thomas is a little busy at the moment," he said. "I have it on good authority he's far too busy to see anyone."

I tapped into the network for an instant, to check the place of Thomas' mind. He was near the far corner of the suite, in his office behind the rooms with the cleans. He wasn't networking but seemed to be alone because I detected no other minds in the room. I had a bad feeling at that moment, and an image of Rain flashed into my mind. I severed the connection. The guard did not take even a step toward me. But his arms uncrossed and he reached for the gun holster at his belt.

"I'm gonna ask you one more time," he said as his hand continued to drift. "Get back on that elevator."

That tore it, tore it straight in half. I accessed the network. The man could shoot me in seconds, but if he did, he would alert everyone. I reached into my mental information catalog, a vast library of irrelevant information. I packed as much as I could into the fastest sort of poison packet. Then I shot it at the guard's unsuspecting mind.

His mentality resonated like that of musician, visible as an outline that hummed in the mental space. His safeguards were nothing special, a simplistic maze of barriers and a few antibodies. Though I didn't have a lot of experience cutting through defenses, I was able to guide my poison packet through the maze to the end. A pair of antibodies surged at my mentality and the packet, but I pushed my cargo past them before I shot back out of the maze.

He folded under the weight of the information, at least for the moment. When I severed the connection he stared vacantly at me, mind overloaded with the forced download. If he had been at all prepared for a network attack I could have been shot before the packet took effect on him. But he hadn't been. He might be under the protection of a rogue star, but she didn't help him.

Yashelia.

With the guard incapacitated by the flood of information and staring vacantly into space, I charged down the hallway toward the office. I ran with a serious lack of sprinters' muscles. Even when I'd been young, I didn't make a fast runner. I was out of breath when I slammed my shoulder into the door of Thomas' office and hurled it wide open.

Within, a glimmer of white blonde hair greeted me. *Damn it.* Yashelia stood with one slender arm extended, pinning Thomas against the wall by the throat. She turned as I entered, and one eye of yellow with red flecks fixed on me.

"So, you are here," she said. "I take it my guard did not inconvenience you much?"

"Let him go," I said. "I don't know what you're after, but I'm pretty sure it isn't Thomas."

"What makes you say that, Jethro?"

"It's because you're looking for someone."

"Perhaps I am. What of it?"

Thomas struggled, both hands working against Yashelia's impervious grip. I gritted my teeth and stared into Yashelia's eye.

"I can tell you where she is."

"She. Who am I looking for?"

"The one thing that connects you to me and Thomas. Rain."

She released her grip on Thomas' throat, and he slumped to the floor, barely able to even slow himself. He disappeared into shadow. Yashelia turned to face me full on. A wound, patterned by angry red lines radiating out from it, was bored into her forehead just over her right eyebrow. She smiled coldly. "Well, well. You are an interesting one, are you not? How did you know?"

"What else changed between today and yesterday," I said. My breath caught. "And she's here. Here in the Mangrove Suite."

"Take me to her," she said.

"Thomas knows where she is. I just know she's here."

Yashelia's arm extended. She grabbed Thomas by his suit collar and dragged him to his feet. "Thomas, lead the way."

He tried to push her arm away, but she did not let him go. Behind me, the guard arrived at the door, having recovered from my mental dump in his mind.

"Matthias," said Yashelia. "Follow us. Keep an eye on these two better than you watched the elevator, please."

The big man grunted but nodded, too.

I turned toward her as Yashelia strode past me, half-dragging, half-pushing Thomas in front of her. Matthias shoved his revolver at my face, barrel first. Then Yashelia caught his eye. He lowered the weapon and let us past. He brought up the rear of the group, following with a sickened expression.

Thomas led the way down the hallway to a door like any other door. He opened it, muscles taut in his face. Yashelia swept inside and I followed, not knowing if she would be angry or not. But I needed to see Rebecca, Rain, what Rebecca had become.

Rain sat on the bed, dressed in a thin button-down shirt and pair of dark pants. Both shirt and pants were far too big for her. She looked up at Yashelia with a vacant expression. The same look in her beautiful eyes as she'd had for me when I'd seen her the previous day. I clenched my fist but felt the barrel of a gun in the small of my back. *Fuck,* Matthias was still right there.

"There you are, my dear." Yashelia let out purring sound. "I missed you, Rebecca."

She drew close to Rain who recoiled with wide eyes.

"They never should have taken you from me. But this time, I won't let them clean you out. Give me your hands, deary." Yashelia reached for Rain's hand, but she recoiled, trying to get away.

"What do you want with her?" I said, no longer registering the threat of Matthias behind me. He clocked me on the back of the skull for my trouble. The steel of the barrel rocked my skull, dazing me and sending pain shooting through my nerves. I stumbled into the room.

Rain screamed. Yashelia did not turn to face me.

"Matthias, kill the men."

My eyes widened as Matthias raised the revolver. His finger eased toward the trigger.

I sent my mentality flying into his mind to delay the inevitable, if only for an instant. I darted through his maze again, no packet prepared, and dove into his poorly-tended mind. He stiffened. I looked over my shoulder just Thomas swept in from the other side.

Matthias grunted and dropped the revolver. Another packing sound, like meat getting tenderized. Matthias slammed into the door frame. I glanced back as he fell to the ground. Yashelia released a cacophonic scream and turned toward me.

"Fucker," Matthias gasped. Thomas kicked him in the head and silenced him.

Thomas picked up his revolver and trained it on Yashelia. I eased to one side to give him a clearer shot and ready to run to get Rain as soon as he fired. Yashelia's scream heightened in pitch, searing my ears, but I refused to cover them. Even if I had, I guessed that as much of the scream was inside my head as was outside it. Rain winced and bowed her head, hands over her ears. I took a step toward Yashelia.

Thomas gritted his teeth and glared at Yashelia. "Leave. Now. Bitch."

The gun might not kill an aeon. They looked human, but their abilities and toughness varied.

She reached out to grab Rain's arm. Rain tried to pull back, but Yashelia's grip was too strong. The pale aeon dragged Rain toward the window. Aeons were tough and could glide on the wind. If Yashelia got outside with Rain, I might never have a chance to see her again.

I dove toward them, seizing a fistful of Yashelia's long coat. The rogue star launched herself and Rain toward the window. Thomas fired. A roar of sound cut through the sound of Yashelia's screeching voice. The bullet went through the arm Yashelia was using to hold Rain.

Ichor, golden in the light from the window, exploded across Rain's face. Yashelia released Rain just as I lost my grip on her coat.

The rogue star hurtled out the window, breaking the glass and the frame, and tearing curtains from their posts. I slid along the floor with the force of her leap, catching up with Rain just as shattered window glass crashed down and out into the air forty stories over he city.

I grabbed Rain and covered her head with my arms and body. The curtain came down on us, along with a heavy pole. It hit my back, sending a shock of pain through me to match hitting the ceiling of the train car earlier that day.

But I held onto Rain. Yashelia's scream faded into the distance. If she really was an aeon, she could survive that fall by creating a wind current like she had done before when she had escaped the train.

I arched my back and pushed the curtain off. Rain sat up and her tongue ran out, lapping up a few droplets of Yashelia's ichor from her lips. Thomas ran over to us just as a light seemed to come on in Rain's eyes.

"Jeth?" She met my gaze.

My eyes were teary, partially from pain, but partially from disbelief. "Rebecca?"

"Call me Rain," she said.

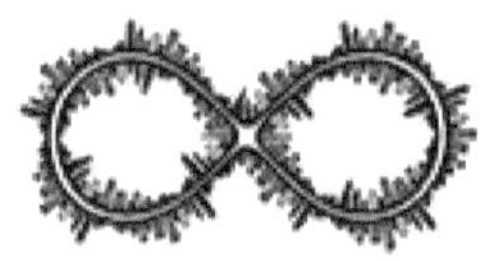

5

UNREGISTERED MEMORY, Elizabeth Ashwood, 12th Floor Restaurant, Lotdel Tower

After a day of distributing data via the local network, Elizabeth waited in the restaurant for Jeth to arrive. She checked her watch a few times. She had not expected him to be this late. Part of her worried he must have gone up to the Mangrove Suite to spend time with the mindless girl he had bought. Part of her didn't want to believe he would do something like that.

The cleans were practically animals. They didn't have any capacity for intellect, or expression, or love. *Could he be so enamored with an animal that he can't see me?* She sighed and sipped her water. She fought the temptation to add a drop of ichor to bolster her diminishing network strength, and then look for him mentally. She did not fight hard.

She reached into her purse and retrieved the bottle she carried there. She loosened the lid and held it over her water. She dripped aeon's blood into the cup. As she raised it to her lips, a shadow crossed the table, blocking out the orange sunset coming through the westward window. Elizabeth hesitated, then looked up into the shining face of Nageddia, keeper of Lotdel Tower.

The aeon wore a soft frown on her dark and finely featured face. Around her shoulders hung a thick robe. Her hands were folded before her. "Elizabeth," she said. "I take it you are missing someone?"

Elizabeth bowed her head to hide her surprised expression as much as out of respect. Nageddia would benefit from increased fame once Elizabeth and Jethro got their new network off the ground. For that reason, she seemed to like them even more than she liked her other tenants.

"Jethro's late."

"You were supposed to share a meal."

Elizabeth nodded.

Nageddia's eyes narrowed. "He is in the Mangrove Suite." A slender boy, one of Nageddia's attendants, approached from one side of the aeon. "Ma'am, I have contacted the purifiers."

"Thank you, William. Tell them to hold back for now."

"Is Jeth in trouble?" Elizabeth asked, unable to stop herself.

"He may be," said Nageddia, "but do not fear. I am merciful."

"Please," said Elizabeth. "He may be acting like a fool, but let me try to contact him before you send someone up there."

"You are brash, Elizabeth." Nageddia's lips formed a small smile. "I understand your concern, but it is the rogue star. Somehow, she breached the security of this tower and made her way to the Mangrove Suite."

Elizabeth had heard over the network about the attack on the train. Her heart skipped a beat. "Could she be after Jeth?"

"This is the second time today they have been in contact." Nageddia turned to the boy. "Tell the purifiers to form a perimeter." The aeon's smile faded completely as she waited for the boy, whose eyes glazed into the network for a few seconds, and then Nageddia returned her solemn gaze to Elizabeth once again. "Please, do not be any more brash tonight. My security is already on their way to the Mangrove Suite."

Elizabeth choked back her first attempt at a reply. She turned and stared down at her plate. *I trust Nageddia. She's a powerful friend, for both me and Jeth. She won't hurt him. I trust her.* She took a deep breath and closed her eyes. "I will take care, Nageddia."

"Nothing in the universe is infallible, but trust in me, Elizabeth."

"I trust you." Her head remained bowed, and she fought back tears. "Thank you."

Nageddia's hands folded together. She swept away from the table where Elizabeth sat. Elizabeth listened to more orders given to the purifiers through the boy, a more secure proxy way to network for an aeon who might be under the scrutiny of another of her own kind.

"Have the purifiers tighten the net," said Nageddia.

Elizabeth's hands trembled, wrinkling the tablecloth. She reached into her mind network. *I have to tell Jeth what's happening. Tell him to be careful.*

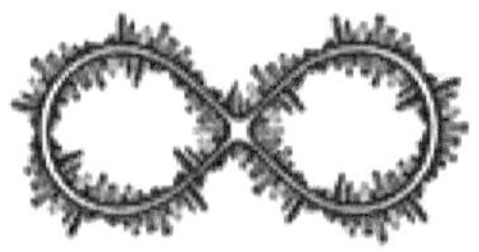

I RELEASED MY EMBRACE of Rain as the veins of light in the room flickered above us, unstable from the shock of Yashelia's passage on the structure of the room. Thomas turned to keep the gun trained on its former owner, Matthias, still lying on the floor. I wished right then that I had seen this coming. I've tinkered with machines before. I've even dipped into some sites to train myself using gun-range records. I'm not a great shot, but I could have done something more.

Thomas glanced at me. "You alright?"

I carefully felt down my side and found a few cuts and tears in my shirt from the broken glass but nothing serious. The only blood I saw on Rain was the few drops of Yashelia's ichor on her cheek.

"We're fine." I rose and helped Rain to her feet. "Thanks, Thomas."

Rain turned her eyes toward Thomas. He was still watching Matthias. Rain walked over to them, careful even in shoes, on the broken glass. She reached for the weapon in Thomas' hand, staring down at Matthias. "He wanted to kill you."

"I know." Thomas sounded numb.

I walked over to them and put my hand on Rain's shoulder. "He's no threat to us now."

Thomas glanced at me, looking past Rain. His eyebrows were up and beneath them his eyes appeared terrified despite his otherwise calm exterior.

"Yashelia is gone," I said. "We just need to call in the security force and explain things."

"And what about me?" said Rain. "I remember being Rebecca. I remember everything."

I swallowed and shook my head. Then I looked at Thomas. "We can't let anyone know she's not clean anymore."

"But why isn't she clean? She definitely was about five minutes ago."

"The blood," said Rain. "The blood of the aeon contains memories, but not all of them complete. This is only temporary."

"How do you know that?" I asked.

"Rebecca studied it. Before the end, she knew."

"You mean, you knew!" I said, unable to hide my anger. "You are Rebecca."

"Maybe," said Rain. "I can't be sure, and even now I'm losing memories. I can feel it."

"How do we stop it?" My fingers tightened on Rain's shoulder. "There has to be a way."

"Do you hear yourself?" Thomas asked. "If the aeons haven't told us how they can restore someone from being cleaned, then they don't want to us to know. It's been two generations since they arrived on Earth. They didn't forget to tell us."

I nodded. "That doesn't mean we shouldn't try to find out."

Rain pulled away from my grip and turned her back on us. "I don't know why they haven't told us," she said. "But Rebecca may have. I can't. I can't reach that memory."

Thomas took a step back from Matthias. "You want to find something that, by the way, probably got Rebecca cleaned in the first place. They'll want to clean us, too, if we go looking for it."

Matthias let out a harsh chuckle from the floor. "You'd deserve it, you bastard. You sell the bodies of cleans for a living."

Thomas's fingers trembled on the gun. "They don't know what they're doing. They only know they enjoy it."

"Yeah, right."

Thomas lowered the barrel of the gun to point at the floor between them. "Shut the fuck up."

"Oh, did I hit a nerve?" Matthias chuckled again. "What's the matter? Gonna shoot me?"

I walked over to Matthias, who lay on his side, looking up at Thomas. Whatever Thomas did, and whatever I might think of it, he didn't deserve to hear this kind of shit from a thug like this one. I walked around Matthias and planted my heel on his shoulder. "You heard him," I said. "Now you can shut up or I can start pressing."

"Don't hurt him," said Rain. "Jeth, don't hurt him."

"Oh, the girl who just woke up is begging you. Jeth, you'd better listen to her. After all, you're gonna want to fuck her later, right?"

My pulse jumped, and the world looked redder than the sunset should make it. I raised my foot. Then I stomped it down on Matthias' shoulder with all the force I could muster. Something *cracked* inside the man, and he screamed out. "Next time you get shot," I said.

A cold breeze from the broken windows answered me.

Then came a clatter of footsteps in the stairwell back near the elevator. I glanced at Thomas and Rain. "If this is security, don't tell them about Rain."

Thomas frowned at me for a long moment, then he nodded.

Rain bowed her head in a long nod. "I don't want to lose these memories."

I paced around in front of Matthias, and then looked down at his face.

Matthias gasped from pain and met my gaze. "If I tell them, they'll clean me. Don't worry, I won't let that happen."

"I bet you won't," I said, fingers clenched. Boots thundered in the hall outside, then a pair of men in white-plated armor with fiery patterned trim, turned the corner, submachine guns at the ready.

I put my hands up immediately as I recognized the purifiers, and I opened my fists. One of them shouted at Thomas to drop the gun. My friend didn't hesitate, though he winced at the volume of the purifier's modulated voice. The pistol clattered to the floor.

Rain stood looking vacant, the cover she needed to maintain. The purifiers stormed into the room. Two more white-armored troopers appeared in the doorway and I knew there were probably even more of them outside. Purifiers never did things half way, or so was their reputation.

"Hands on your head." The lead purifier trained his weapon on me. I obeyed. Thomas did the same.

He nodded his masked head. Another one kept his gun on me while the leader moved on to Matthias. The thug on the ground looked up at the purifiers. "You got me, you bastards," he said through wheezes of pain.

I may have messed him up more with that stomp on his shoulder than I initially thought.

The purifier leader hesitated for a moment, seemingly doing nothing as Matthias glared at him. He had accessed the mental network. "Convict Matthias Tannenmoore, on your feet." One of the other purifiers dragged Matthias up, where he looked as though he might fall. The leader turned to me, networked for an instant, then said, "Jethro Gall and Thomas Fenstein, the team will escort you and your clean downstairs."

I glanced at Rain. She returned my gaze with a vacant stare. Purifiers led us out of the room and to the elevator.

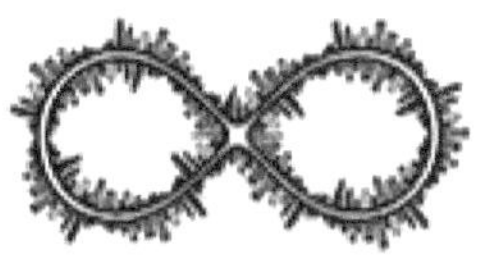

UNREGISTERED MEMORY, Elizabeth Ashwood, First Floor Lobby, Lotdel Tower

The crowd of people behind Elizabeth in the tiled lobby of Lotdel Tower murmured rumors as to why they had been sent downstairs. Without Nageddia present to reply, they would get no solid answers. Elizabeth had no plans to tell what she had heard in the restaurant. Her eyes moved side to side and she noted about half of the people she could see were networking, obviously seeking more answers. Her eyes focused on the elevator doors. *Jeth needs to be safe. I know he's done something stupid, buying that clean, but why did things go so crazy so fast?*

The doors to the elevator opened. Elizabeth's breath caught, but instead of Jeth, Nageddia and her small entourage of servants, including the young boy from earlier, emerged. Nageddia swept out of the elevator behind a pair of bodyguards without visible weapons. Elizabeth scowled at her feet, trying not to blurt out her question for the aeon who owned Lotdel Tower.

She's doing her best to help Jeth. She has to be trying. My job is to remain calm.

Elizabeth evened out her expression and then looked up from the floor. Nageddia stopped just a meter or two from the crowd where her guards formed a perimeter to keep the people back. Nageddia pressed her palms together, redness and dark spots of ichor-giving wounds visible on the back of her hands.

"My people," said Nageddia. "The rogue star has invaded this tower." A ripple of soft voices ran through the crowd. "Remain calm. For your safety, please remain here until the purifiers secure the higher floors. The rogue star will not attack you here, and the purifiers will keep you safe."

Fear ran through Elizabeth, not as a chill, but as a fiery wave, one mingled with her anger. *How would Nageddia's forces deal with the rogue star, as well as the people who the monster attacked?*

"One of the other tenants of this building encountered the rogue star earlier today on a train. Please, be cautious." Nageddia turned to the boy whose eyes were glazed with ichor. Her voice lowered in volume, but Elizabeth could still hear her thanks to being at the front of the crowd. Nageddia said, "William, where are they?"

"Network indicates they are on their way down."

"Good," said Nageddia.

Elizabeth stared at the aeon and the boy and waited. A *clank* drew Elizabeth's attention to the elevator as its doors opened again. A team of purifiers in their shocking white and red armor escorted four other people out of the elevator. Thomas Fenstein, Jeth's friend, stood beside a black man in a suit and handcuffs with a growing purple bruise on the side of his head. Behind those two walked a beautiful woman with tanned brown skin and dark hair in baggy clothes, and beside her, Jeth, with bloody streaks down one side of his shirt. Elizabeth's eyes moved from Jeth to woman beside him. Her eyes looked empty, a clean.

The group made their way to Nageddia, and Elizabeth stared at them as the group of purifiers dispersed except for the team leader who stood beside the four. *Jeth, what have you gotten yourself into?* Elizabeth stepped forward from the crowd.

Nageddia's eyes locked on her, jaw set. "Stay where you are, Miss Ashwood."

Elizabeth froze at the edge of the perimeter. She met Nageddia's gaze and tried not to show the fear she felt. "Please, don't make me wait to see if my partner is alright."

Nageddia's expression softened just a little. "For a moment. Come forward."

Elizabeth bowed her head and walked past the guards to Nageddia and the four. She looked up and found Jeth's eyes on her. She turned toward him. "Are you alright, Jeth?" she asked.

"Yeah." Jeth nodded to her.

Elizabeth nodded to him, but she couldn't help her brow creasing.

Thomas glanced over his shoulder at Jeth but said nothing. Nageddia motioned with a hand, and one of the guards gestured for Elizabeth to move back. Then the team of purifiers regrouped and took the four of them through the crowd, past Elizabeth, and out into the vein-lit night outside the tower's doors. Elizabeth watched them go. *You had better tell me everything, Jeth. I can't keep worrying about you like I'm doing now.* She swallowed hard as the doors closed behind the purifiers.

6

THEY DROVE US NORTH in a pair of armored cars, but we didn't go far. Interrogation at the purifier hall six blocks from Lotdel Tower surprised me with its speed. The purifiers knew we didn't know anything. Except for Matthias. Despite the thug's insinuations earlier, I didn't like to think what would become of him.

I told my story to a recording memeotect, omitting the part where Rain had regained her memory from Yashelia's blood. If they caught me, I could be in serious trouble, but I kept those thoughts tight to my center to keep them from radiating out to the memeotects in the building.

Security released Thomas, Rain, and I just before midnight and gave us all a ride back to Lotdel Tower. I was starving, having eaten nothing since I left the office after lunch. The restaurants were closed, and I had little left in my apartment. Luckily, Thomas kept a cold box in the Mangrove Suite to store food for his cleans. Rain and I took the elevator up with him. On the remnants of the day's ichor I reached out and checked for reports on the rogue star called Yashelia.

I had shared the name. Why not? I had not said I thought she was an aeon because that could be dangerous. Of course, the authorities would find her home garden soon if she was an aeon. I delved into a stack of memory that looked like a mountain of light and began rifling through records kept from earlier encounters with previous rogue stars as well as those with Yashelia leading up to when I met her on the train.

According to records, rogue stars usually appeared in groups, clusters of nonhuman agents from outside the city. Most rogue stars went unidentified even after being killed or driven off. I didn't find a single record of one taken alive. Whoever designated Yashelia as a rogue star clearly wanted her dead, and only the most respected aeons could assign the designation such that the other aeons would distribute the information through the networks they controlled.

The elevator reached the Mangrove Suite. The place was dark and closed, the cleans locked in their rooms after the purifiers had sent the clients away. Thomas led Rain and I down a hall opposite the main rooms to a lounge overlooking the shadowy canal and the parks to the southwest. He hit the light switch and the veins in the ceiling pulsed with blue power supplied from some heart far away.

I sat across from Rain, each of us in a large easy chair, as Thomas went to the cold box in the next room to get us something to eat. Tired, I quickly began to doze as we waited. Rain, who looked more alert now that no purifiers could see us, turned to me. "Don't fall asleep, Jeth," she said.

"Why not?"

"I don't know if I'll be here when you wake up."

I frowned at her, then lurched forward in my easy chair. I put my hands on my knees. "How much do you remember?"

"I remember a garden. A tall tree of stone at its center."

"Sounds like you're thinking of an aeon's garden. They always keep at least one stone tree."

"It's stranger than that," she said. "This stone tree has grown wild. Branches snare and cross with each other. I watched the whole garden overgrow. She told me not to worry about it, but I knew something was wrong."

"Slow down for a second is, *she* Yashelia?"

"Yes."

"Can you remember where this garden was?"

"Here in the east, west of Lotdel Tower." She pointed out the window at the darkened city. "It's by water."

"A canal?" I said.

"Or a reservoir. Maybe a lake."

"Standing water?"

"I think so." She put both hands to her temples. "It's getting hazier."

"Hang on. Thomas will be back any second now. He knows about cleans. Maybe he can help."

Rain glared at me from under her hands. "No human can help me with this. Only the aeon who cleaned me has that power."

"Was it Yashelia?"

"Yes." Rain pushed herself up from her chair and stood. She paced to the dark window, her skin glowing in the blue lights of the room. "But how can we find her?"

"It seemed like she was looking for you," I said.

"She wanted to take me back. I can't remember why."

"How did Rebecca know Yashelia?" I asked.

Rain turned from the window. Her eyes gleamed with tears, the first tears I had ever seen on someone who had been cleaned. "Rebecca. She was in over her head. She was afraid of Yashelia before it happened."

"Is that all you can remember?" I tried to sound as gentle as I could.

She took a step toward me. Shadows darkened her face. Her eyes glittered within the darkness. "That's what I remember." Her hands clenched into fists. "Jeth, I don't like being seen like this. I'm fading."

I stared at her for a moment. Then I tore my gaze away and nodded. "I'm sorry. I wish I could do more. I *will* do more. Promise."

Her footsteps approached, and she sat down on one large arm of my easy chair. Her legs dangled over the side opposite me. I turned and looked up at her. She shook her head. "I know you will, but don't get yourself hurt, Jeth. Rebecca would never want that."

I took a deep breath. "And what about Rain?"

Her eyes closed. "Rain never knows what she wants."

My hand found Rain's on the arm of the easy chair. She sat like a statue. The door to the rest of the suite opened and Thomas came in with a plate of food in each hand, his shadow cast in blue lights from the room and yellow ones from the hallway.

"I hope you're not too tired, Jeth. I've got to tell you something."

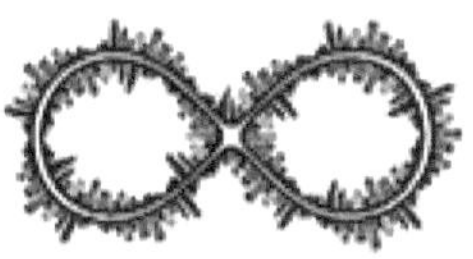

UNREGISTERED MEMORY, Ryan Carter, The Marya Building

Not many analysts got awakened by purifiers for work in the dead of night. Once he recovered from the shock, Ryan considered himself lucky to be in such demand. The rogue star they called Yashelia had struck inside Lotdel Tower, in the domain of a law-abiding and well-connected aeon. Now, security and purifier elements would be working together to catch her.

Ryan stretched as he followed the masked and armored purifier officer down the dimly lit hall from his apartment. They took an elevator to the ground floor where another squad of purifiers who wore Teloite Lawkeeper emblems on their chests met them by the doors inside the lobby. "Analyst Carter," said one of the purifiers in a firm feminine voice. "Are you prepared?"

"I'll need ichor, and a good sensocycler to assist me." *You guys had better pay well, too, for getting me up in the middle of the night.*

"We have both on location for you," said the woman. "I'm Commander De Vries. You answer to me for this op."

Ryan saluted, one fist to his heart and the other arm locked to his side as aeon security forces demanded. "Thank you for the opportunity, commander."

She returned the gesture with a lightning fast movement. Then she waved the other purifiers toward the door. "Move people, we've got a ticking clock."

Ryan hurried out the door with the others. Outside the doors, they were met by cold night air on their way to the armored car. Only the richest aeons could afford this kind of force just to pick up an intelligence specialist. *I'm flattered. Flattered and curious.* He climbed into the back of the armored car with the purifiers. He sat in the middle of a row of seats along the side of the vehicle. One of the purifiers, it might have been De Vries, but Ryan couldn't tell thanks to the dark and the armor, handed him a sealed metal canister.

Ryan cracked the top with a twist of the cap, then drank the ichor within the little bottle like a shot. His world swam with shadows and shapes. Ryan put a hand to his forehead but grinned as his senses expanded. His consciousness accelerated, sharpened, and spread like ice on the surface of a lake in winter.

As the initial rush faded, Ryan delved into his own mind, clearing his head of all the emotional data that could inhibit analysis. The eyes of his mind looked around the bright hills and valleys of the network while those of his body closed in the dark. On either side of him sat a memetically trained purifier, both with active minds. One of them was indeed Commander De Vries, evidenced by the public packet Ryan received when his mentality peered at hers.

He skimmed the little document, picked out a few details, and then cross-checked them to verify her identity. Things checked out, and one other element became clear. Her purifier unit operated under a great aeon called Sudhatho, a Teloite warlord. *Interesting,* Ryan thought, *but it makes sense the Teloites want to stop a rogue star.*

The armored car rumbled through iron and wire gates and stopped in front of an office building surrounded by a perimeter of fences and walls. He climbed out, aware of the security officers and purifiers all around him. Commander De Vries led him into the building through double doors. Officers saluted him and De Vries as they passed.

She led him into a square room with a vacant circular table in the center. In each corner of the room sat a small human form on a chair. They appeared to be children dozing, but Ryan guessed differently. These four were banks, humanlike bodies grown and birthed using surrogate mothers to house data, the memories of others. *I hope they were never real people,* Ryan thought, *but that is a possibility.*

De Vries motioned for Ryan to take a seat at the table. He obeyed.

"Search for Yashelia." De Vries paced around the far side of the table. "We have all the data we have accumulated about her and the other most recent rogue star in these four. Everything you need should be accessible."

Ryan nodded, but his eyes remained on De Vries. "And the sensocycler I requested?"

"He should report here shortly. Be as discreet with any details you learn from these four banks. They are the property of a power you do not want to cross." She circled the table and walked back toward the door. "Acquaint yourself with as much information as you can, and contact me when you've found anything at all that seems promising."

"Understood."

"Good. Don't let us down, Carter." De Vries marched to the door and left for the hall outside. A moment later, the door opened again and a heavily set man with red hair and a black coat instead of a uniform entered.

"You must be our new analyst," said the man. He sat down in a seat beside Ryan. "Carter, is it?"

Ryan nodded. "And you're the sensocycler I requested?"

"Conner Kohl." The man held out a thick hand and they shook. "You find the data, I'll keep my eyes peeled," Kohl said.

"Glad to hear it." Ryan released the man's hand and ran his hands over his temples. "Let's get started."

"Could be a long shift." Kohl smirked. "Finally, I get to work with someone serious."

In answer, Ryan closed his eyes and delved back into the network.

IN THE LOUNGE AT THE Mangrove Suite, Thomas handed a plate to me and the other to Rain, who sat on the arm of my easy chair, then he took the chair across from us. He took a deep breath. "You two have caused a lot of trouble, but don't worry I'm not about to turn you in as long as we're open about everything from this point forward. What do you know about Yashelia, Jeth?"

I shrugged. "Not much. I ran into her on the train to work yesterday. I have no idea why she went after Rain, but she knew who I was on that train."

Rain's hand went stiff beneath mine. She raised her eyes and looked at Thomas. "She was after me."

"Why?" asked Thomas.

She scowled at the floor. "I don't remember why. Not anymore."

"Her memories are fading," I said.

Thomas took a deep breath. "I was worried something like that might happen."

"You were worried?" I glanced from Rain to Thomas.

He nodded. "The Mangrove Suite is my brothel, but you've never asked me what I did with the proceeds. Why I buy new cleans every year."

I started to speak, but hesitated. Ever since I moved into Lotdel Tower I had spent as little time thinking about this floor as I could. Being friends with Thomas had not helped with that. I shook my head. "What are you trying to say, Thomas?"

"I've been connected to a group. They run experiments on cleans, try to figure out what happens to the information aeons take from them, and what cleans really are."

"A group. Scientists?" I frowned. "Why haven't you ever mentioned this to me before?"

"I figured you wouldn't like it. They take a few cleans at a time for some credits, but they also share their results with me." Thomas folded his hands together and hunched forward. "Everyone knows ichor overdose is what gets people cleaned. But my contacts think it's more than that. The aeon that does the cleaning is tied to every human they've cleaned somehow."

"Do they not know how yet?" I asked.

"They don't know, Jeth."

"It was Yashelia's ichor," I said. "Just a few drops."

Rain nodded. "I tasted it. And I knew she was the one who cleaned me."

My eyes narrowed.

Thomas whistled. "That could explain why she was looking for her."

"I don't want to lose my mind," Rain said, "but I can feel it happening."

I reached for her wrist. She slipped off the chair and stood up. "Let me look at you while I can." She turned toward me. "Jeth, why did you come to this city?"

Thomas settled back in his chair and looked at me. I looked up at Rain's face. "I couldn't just stay in the valley after you left. I came here to be a memeotect."

"You did it." She smiled, a slight curve of the lips. "I hope you're happy."

"I'll be happier once we get you back."

"Jeth, what are you going to do?" Thomas asked.

My eyes met Rain's. "I want to find Yashelia." My stomach growled, and I looked down at my plate. "But first, I'm going to eat. We're all going to need to stay sharp."

Thomas nodded.

Rain looked at her plate of food. "I don't know how long I'll last," she murmured, "but you're right." She looked at me. "I want to wake up again."

I looked at her face. Her smiled had gone as quickly as it had appeared. Thomas sighed but with a hint of a grin on his face. "Nothing but trouble."

We ate.

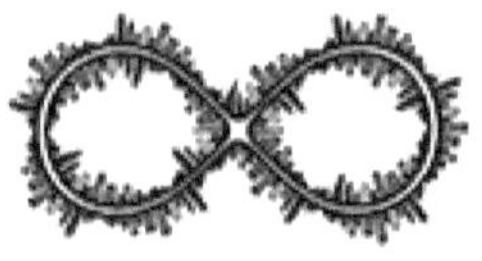

7

I WOKE WITH AN ACHE in my back and swung my legs out of bed. The covers already lay piled in at the foot of the bed, and the air was chill in my apartment. I stood, walked over to the dresser by my windows where the beginnings of morning sunlight filtered through, and then put on a pair of blue jeans. Only then did I realize the shower was running in the bathroom. *Rain.*

She had wanted to stay in my apartment the past night, but I did not remember more after our embrace on the couch in the living room after she told me she was afraid to sleep. Even as dawn crept over the city, and I turned from the window, I hoped Thomas and Rain had been wrong, though I knew she had felt her memories fading.

I slipped on a heavily woven shirt and walked down the hallway past the bathroom and into my tiny kitchen. I filled my flask with ichor from a plastic container I kept in my all but empty cold box. Footsteps behind me made me turn. Rain stood naked at the end of the hallway. A few droplets of water glistened in her hair and a sheen of moisture gleamed on her light brown skin. I set the flask on the counter and stared at her.

"Rain?" I said. "Are you alright?"

"Are you?" Her eyes never met mine, but I glimpsed them, bright and vacant as she turned away.

Were it not for the strange question she had asked me I would have guessed she was completely clean again. I felt numb.

"I'm fine. Rain, do you know who I am?"

She tossed her hair back and took a step toward me. "Jeth?"

"Yes. That's my name." I felt tight as she approached me.

Her hips shifted and her head tilted back. She looked up at my face. "You seem familiar," she said. "But I don't. I don't remember why."

"That's alright." I put a palm to my forehead and took a deep breath. "Are you hungry?"

"No. Full." Her vacant gaze moved from my face down my body to my waist. "I feel the same as you."

Heat raced to my face. I grimaced. "Please, let's not talk about that."

"I don't want to talk either." She put her hands to the top of my pants. Her fingers ran along the inside of the waistband from side to front. I stepped back and banged into the counter behind me. Her fingers fell out of my pants. "What's wrong?"

"I can't." *I will not take advantage of her. She would understand if she remembered more than my name.*

"You seem ready."

"I can't!"

She drew back, a frown of confusion and hurt forming on her face. She shuddered. I tried to swallow with a dry mouth. Rain backed away, eyes downcast. She prowled around the kitchen counter and into the living room. I turned my head after a glimpse of her from behind. I couldn't let this get out of hand. I still needed to restore her mind.

I took a flask of ichor and went back to my bedroom. There, I put on my coat, and then I dug into my closet and found the twelve gauge shotgun I had practiced with once. I found a few shells for it, then hid everything in cardboard box under my bed. I didn't want to be weaponless if something happened or we located Yashelia. Part of me doubted the shotgun would do much to her. Another part of me wanted to think I could at least get more ichor from her that way.

The third part of me wanted to throw up at both thoughts. I walked through the living room, passing Rain where she had mercifully covered herself with a blanket on the couch. I locked the apartment door on the way out. She glared at me as I left. I took a deep breath and hit the down button for the elevator.

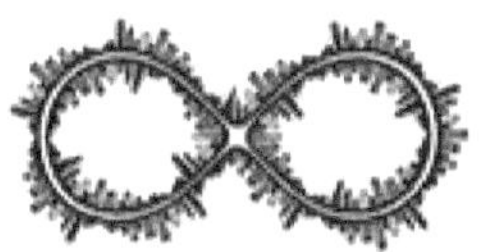

THOMAS WAS ON THE ELEVATOR when it arrived. He nodded to me.

"How is she?" he asked.

I stepped inside and scowled at my feet. "She's clean."

"It wore off?"

"Yeah. She barely remembers anything."

"But she remembers something?"

"My name. Maybe a few mannerisms. Cleans have recall too, Thomas, but only simple stuff."

"Jeth, this a lot better than I would have expected from a single drop of Yashelia's ichor."

I looked up at him, only just focused on his face. "You sure that's the only ichor that will work?"

Thomas shrugged with both shoulders. "Positive."

I sighed and leaned against the wall of the elevator. "That helps a little." We went down three floors, and then the door opened again. Elizabeth stepped inside.

A relieved smile formed on her face. "You two. You're alright!"

"Yeah," I said, my mouth suddenly dry again. "Security only wanted to talk to us."

"Are you going down for breakfast?"

"Yeah," I said.

"I was just in the library looking up some things." Her smile slipped away as she looked at my face. "Jeth, what happened? You aren't telling me everything."

"That clean I bought at the market." The elevator reached the twelfth floor and the door opened into the hall outside the restaurant.

I stepped out with the others and leaned close to Elizabeth. "She remembered something after the attack yesterday."

"Remembered?" She frowned, eyes narrowing. "Did she recognize you?"

"Yes," I said. Thomas paced evenly past Elizabeth and went on to the restaurant. I put a hand on Elizabeth's shoulder. "I'll tell you more when we're sure—"

Thomas turned toward us and gave a thumbs up.

"Now is fine," I said. "Basically a clean's memory can be restored for a limited time by drinking the ichor of the aeon that cleaned her."

Elizabeth's eyes went from narrow, to wide, to wider, but her frown remained. "You can't be serious, Jeth."

"I don't know much about this, but I'm not lying." I glanced at Thomas, who stood by the entrance of the restaurant, arms folded. "Look, I'll let you see the memory. I'll show you."

"Alright, Jeth." Elizabeth shook her head. "Show me, and we'll see if I believe you."

"You know I've never been good at building false memories."

Her lips pressed together. "We'll see." She turned and we walked into the restaurant together, joined by Thomas on the way.

The smell of bacon drifted through the air, mingled with the fresh scent of morning from the open windows. We dished up and took a booth. I felt a lack of sleep as I looked out into the misty air outside, rising from Bailey Court Garden. My eyes drifted over the treetops and foliage where birds chirped and circled above orange and brown leaves.

Elizabeth turned, sipped from her bottle of ichor, and then set it on the table. "Show me, Jeth."

I took a swallow of ichor from my flask. Sensory information flared through me. Bird calls sounded sharper, the bacon smelled more delicious. I reached out a willowy mental branch and touched the tough exterior of Elizabeth's mind. A mind can appear small on the network, but such is the fractal nature of the mental world one sees more the closer one gets.

Elizabeth's mind appeared as a crystal of pale blue and glimmering white. As I drew closer, the patterns of lace-like tendrils and frost fingers curved around the edges of the crystal became visible in my mind's eye. A bass note accompanied my closeness to her, droning low and completely inaudible to my actual ears. The temperature seemed to drop as I reached out and touched the crystal. At first, I noticed just a slight chill, then Elizabeth pulled me in.

The shock of entering her mental space sent a message of winter cold through my brain. If I hadn't known better I would have worried my synapses might freeze from this plunge into an icy world of logic and precision. I glimpsed a memory of an old mechanic's workshop with the silhouette of the city's towers thrown up against the distant skyline. A little girl with a face like Elizabeth's sat on the curb outside. She turned toward my vantage point, which I realized was the remembered vision of Elizabeth herself. The little girl had tears in her eyes.

Elizabeth pushed me back. Her cold fingers rummaged through my memories from the past few days. Hope and pain blended as images of Rain appeared before my eyes. First she was dancing in the clean market, a frozen image with one leg raised, knee bent and ankle held to her thigh like a ballerina in a spin. I wanted to hide her, to not show Elizabeth this sight. Yet the image remained.

"Jeth," Elizabeth's voice entered through the network. *"Don't pull away from me."*

I did not reply but tried to relax and still my desperation. She delved past the image of Rain and our mentalities arrived together at the Mangrove Suite on the next day. Yashelia had Thomas by the throat when I rushed in. I blotted out my remembered words. My pulse accelerated. Elizabeth and I followed the group of memories down the hallway to Rain's room, and we watched the window shatter. We watched as Rain licked the blood from her lips.

Her eyes changed, and she said, "Jeth?"

"Rebecca?"

"Call me Rain."

The image froze with her face imprinted on mine and Elizabeth's eyes. Then we flashed forward, racing through the next moments. Numb from the cold of Elizabeth's mind, I watched as we took the elevator down to the ground floor. Watched as Elizabeth approached. Then Elizabeth pushed me back and ejected me from her mind.

I sat before my breakfast in a daze. "Do you believe me now?"

Shakily, she put her hands in her lap. "I-I believe you, Jeth. I just don't understand. Why was that aeon looking for Rain?"

"I don't know," I said.

Thomas sighed and leaned back in his seat in the booth. "Yeah, but we all know she was the one who cleaned Rain in the first place."

Elizabeth glanced sideways at him. "Why would an aeon want anything to do with a clean? I don't get it at all."

"Because cleans don't have memories?" I scowled at Elizabeth. "It's possible we're wrong about that too."

"Now, don't go that far," said Thomas. "We don't have the facts."

I folded my arms, but nodded nonetheless. "It's not the facts I'm worried about. It's the leftover memories." I looked down at my plate, suddenly without an appetite to eat anything.

"Either way, people need to know what we know about aeons and ichor." Elizabeth leaned back in her seat, legs crossed halfway under the table. "Jeth, this is the sort of thing a human-managed network would be perfect for revealing."

Thomas shook his head. "That's not a survival plan. I don't think you realize how much the aeons have worked to keep this from people. My contacts don't even know this much."

"We'll find Yashelia first," I said with what I hoped was an even gaze leveled at Elizabeth. "Then we'll find a way to get the truth out."

Elizabeth's brow furrowed and she pursed her lips. At last, she nodded.

A loud hum from outside drew my attention to the westward windows of the restaurant. A sleek shape unlike anything I had ever seen before, but which somewhat resembled one of the light vessels I knew the aeons from the seaside portions of the megalopolis used to cross the sea, hovered over the street. The vessel was some twenty meters long and tipped on each long side by spherical blue-glowing flight units. Light veins pulsed along the otherwise sleek surface like trails of azure lava in a volcanic mountainside. I stared at the shape until my eyes burned from the brightness, then looked away, blinking.

"What is that?" Elizabeth asked.

"I have no idea." Thomas whistled. "A chariot of the gods?"

I glanced at him. "You wouldn't consider aeons gods, would you?"

He shook his head. "Some people do."

Elizabeth drew in a breath. "There are temples in every district of this city for believers, but that—" She looked toward the light vessel, "that belongs to no god. It's a ship of Sudhatho's fleet, you can tell by the odd design."

"Sudhatho?" I said, still staring at the vessel.

"He's a greater aeon." Elizabeth tore her eyes away from the flying ship. "He owns security forces all over the city."

I swallowed, and then glanced at her. "Security?"

"Give me some time. I'll do my best to find out why he's here." Her eyes glazed over with network access.

I reached out and touched her arm to stop her. "Wait."

Her eyes returned to normal and fixed on me. "What is it?"

"I'm going downstairs. I'll try to find out what they're doing outside the network."

"Why?"

I turned to face the window where the ship descended over the street. A pair of purifier armored cars rolled through beneath it. "It looks like they're taking this real seriously. I feel like it's got something to do with Shelly."

"Shelly?" Thomas raised an eyebrow.

"Yashelia." I smirked. "We can't go around calling her that long name all the time."

Thomas put a hand to one side of his neck. "I hope I never have to meet her again, but I'll help you find her, Jeth. Just be careful."

"Yes," said Elizabeth. "Things could be dangerous down there."

"I know." I stood up. "I'll try to stay out of trouble."

"Really try." Elizabeth picked up her cup of ichor. "I'll keep an eye on you."

"Thanks. Both of you, thanks." I turned from the table and left the restaurant for the hall and then the elevator. As the doors closed with me inside I thought for a moment not to go down, but instead to go back upstairs and try to wait things out. Then I thought of Rain in my apartment, her hungry eyes and reaching fingers. I shuddered and took the elevator to the ground floor.

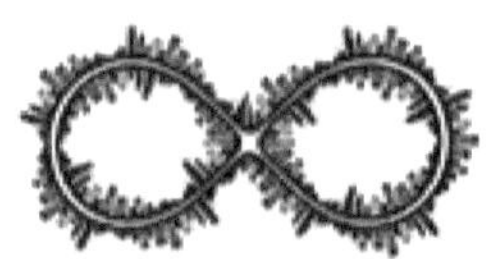

I CROSSED THROUGH THE entryway of Lotdel Tower marching like a soldier. Ichor still infused my senses if I concentrated, and I knew I had network access for at least next eight hours. As I reached the doors, I hesitated and looked out through the glass at the camp set up on the corner of Bailey Court Garden, across the street from Lotdel Tower. Sudhatho's light vessel hung over the rooftops, still not low enough for a human to exit the ship, but aeons could float on the air.

If Sudhatho had come here himself, he could be on the ground. I made a mental note of that fact, remembering the pain of my encounter with Yashelia on the train, and then pushed the door open. The blue lights of its flight systems cast my shadow on the pavement as I walked across the street toward the garden. Overhead, the sky was filled with clouds.

The dead leaves on trees in Bailey Court looked white under the lights of the ship. My mind hummed with a network buzz. I made my way inward to connect mentally with Elizabeth's mental packet. She had sent me an image of a towering, pale-skinned, golden-eyed male aeon. He wore a white cloak with a black collar. It was labeled with Sudhatho. I frowned as I thought over the image of the great aeon. What would he be doing here except looking for a rogue star? *Yashelia.*

And if he finds Yashelia first he could kill her, and if that happens, Rebecca will be lost forever. I made my way to the edge of the garden, bathed in blue light. Gray autumn clouds rolled by overhead, and I heard a loud voice behind me.

"Sudhatho, to what do I owe this honor?" Nageddia said.

I turned to see the aeon that owned Lotdel Tower and her entourage making their way down the street toward a party of purifiers. At the center of the group of purifiers stood a mirror of the image of the pale aeon Elizabeth had just sent over the network. Sudhatho strode out from the center of his purifiers, well over two meters tall and clearly visible over their heads. He swept his cloak back with one arm and put his bloody, wound-marked fist to his heart. He faced Nageddia.

"Little sister," said Sudhatho in a rumbling voice that filled the street. "Thank you for meeting me so promptly."

Nageddia's gaze moved over Sudatho and his entourage, and then fixed on me at the street corner beyond them. Her buzz of alert reached me over the network. *"Jethro, please come here,"* she said in my mind.

I did not dare defy her, especially not with all the purifiers and a greater aeon nearby. I stepped out into the street and walked toward Nageddia. Sudhatho raised an eyebrow as he noticed me. "What is this man doing here, Nageddia?" he asked.

"He is one of my tenants," said Nageddia. "And he encountered the rogue star last night."

Sudhatho's gold eyes moved deliberately. He looked me up and down. His eyes only closed for a moment as he accessed his network. "Jethro Gall," he said. "That wasn't the first time you met the rogue star, was it."

"No," I said as steadily as I could while I kept walking toward Nageddia. "She was on a train, and I recognized her from there."

Aeons have incredible command of ichor and network powers. Sudhatho appeared to be exceptional even by those standards. I felt a pressure on my mind, vast, but momentary. Then the pressure moved away. I sighed with relief as what I guessed was Sudhatho's mental attention moved away from me. Nageddia turned toward me.

"What is it, Jethro?"

I shook my head. "I was curious about the ship." I turned toward Sudhatho. "But now I see why its here."

"Why do you think?" asked Sudhatho in a calm, rhythmic voice, his eyes locked on my face.

I took a deep breath. "You're here to hunt the rogue star."

"You are a clever human." Sudhatho turned to Nageddia. "Make sure he stays out of trouble. The rest of your tenants too."

"I always aim for safety. Jethro, please go back inside. It will be safer for everyone."

I nodded. "As you wish, Nageddia." I obeyed in my actions, walked toward the doors with my head down. I knew already I needed to find another way out of Lotdel Tower, and was doubly sure I needed to find Yashelia before Sudhatho could locate her.

Sudden pressure made me clutch my temple. Sudhatho's voice echoed from behind me. "Stay safe, human."

I limped inside. My head ached. I took the elevator back up to my apartment where Rain awaited.

I PULLED THE DOOR OF my apartment open and stepped inside. Light streamed through the living room window onto the couch where Rain lay curled, arms folded around herself. She looked up at me as the door closed behind me.

"Jeth?" her face lit up. "Are you ready yet?"

I took a deep breath. "No, Rain. I'm not. Please don't ask me again."

Her face fell and she climbed off the couch, still naked from the shower.

I averted my eyes from her beautiful form. "Please, put something on. We need to go back upstairs."

Her eyes glistened with tears. I'd never heard of a clean crying. Maybe the leftover memories from Yashelia's ichor meant she still had emotions more like ordinary humans.

She turned from me and walked to the chair on which her clothes from the previous night were scattered. I couldn't help but watch. To think the girl who had worn a shawl every day in the Green Valley would walk like that without any clothes on. I felt heat rising and turned away from her while she dressed.

She finished putting on the baggie pants and shirt Thomas had gotten for her, and then turned toward me. "Upstairs?" she said.

I turned toward her and nodded. "The Mangrove Suite. You can stay there."

"Thomas won't mind?"

"I don't think he will. Come on."

Rain followed me out the door and down the hall. I felt a twinge of irritation at how long it took the elevator to arrive. No one was on it, which was a mercy. We rode the elevator to the Mangrove Suite and stepped out. Thomas was at the front desk, talking to the two young cleaners he employed. He ushered them away as Rain and I approached.

"Jeth," he said. "What's up?"

I met his eyes with mine. "Rain can't stay at my place."

He nodded. "Awkward, huh?"

"Very."

"Well, I can keep a room for her, but she already cost me one spare so I'll have to shuffle things around."

"It won't be for long." I took Rain by the arm led her around the counter. "Rain," I said. "Please, stay here for a while. Listen to Thomas until I come back."

She nodded without a word. Her eyes narrowed and she looked down at the floor.

Thomas patted her on the shoulder. "Don't worry, we'll keep you out of trouble." He looked past Rain to me. "Jeth, what's the plan?"

"I'm going to search the network for Shelly."

"You really shouldn't call her that."

"Think of it as a codename."

"Like a spy in old books?"

"Yeah, just like that." I forced a smile. "Thomas, I can't thank you enough."

"No," he said. "You can't." He grinned. "Now get out there and do what you gotta do."

I nodded, and then left Rain with him at the desk while I headed for the elevator. I felt the weight of the ichor in the flask at my side. I had work to do, and a monster to track down.

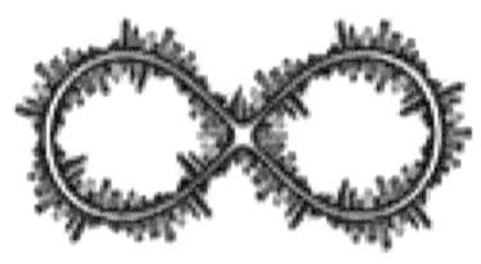

8

I SPENT THE NEXT DAY searching the glittering lights and hummed mental notes of the networks for Yashelia, doing just enough work to keep Omasoa from calling me into the office. Alternately, I spent time mentally sailing over the city and plumbing the depths of the unconscious banks, but turned up little beyond what the news networks filled in for me.

During that time, Sudhatho's troops expanded the net around Lotdel Tower, and people were allowed to come and go again. Three days after I had brought Rain to the Mangrove Suite for the first time, I went down to Bailey Court Garden and walked the rows of trees that looked more and more bare of leaves. As I walked, I tried to get my head around the problem.

Yashelia was hiding somewhere in the city, and even Sudhatho's army of purifiers and security forces could not uncover her location. What chance did I have? I thought of Ryan Carter and how he once told me that this sort of hunt could go on for months. Only when the trail was ice cold could a safety be declared. By then the rogue star would be gone. This time my chances of restoring Rebecca would go with her.

I stopped before a large tree and gazed up at its multicolored heights. I knew something about Yashelia that the aeons had not acknowledged. Yashelia was an aeon, not a typical rogue star. She might be mad, but she had the five wounds and all the other powers. She had a human accomplice before. Could someone else be hiding her? I frowned at the tree. All my network diving had been fruitless. Perhaps because I had been looking for the wrong thing.

My legs carried me deeper into the garden, toward the private part where the trees were still green, nourished by some unseen source despite the gray sky and oncoming winter. I walked on a path between tightly-packed trees, closer and closer to the center of the dense wood. A tree stood at the end of the path some thirty meters off, surrounded by a small clearing.

The tree was anything but small, though. It climbed toward the sky, taller than all the others in this part of the garden. Clean-cut spots where branches had been trimmed ringed the trunk at every level. The branches that had not been trimmed completely spread out higher up, covered in leaves of an unnaturally green color. Even those branches were kept tended by Nageddia's cleans. I'd seen it before, from about this same distance. Most everyone who walked these paths would look at it at least once if they made it this far into the park.

I walked closer, gradually aware of the shapes that moved in the clearing around the tree, humanoid and lithe. Cleans. I hesitated where the path entered the clearing and gazed upward. Above me, the branches of the tree trembled with a chill breeze. Not one impossible leaf fell, though, despite the season.

Someone approached along the path behind me. I looked back and found Elizabeth, her coat bundled around herself, making her way toward me. I nodded to her.

She raised her head. "What are you doing out here?" she asked.

I glanced up at the tree. "Thinking," I said. "Even the smallest aeon parks have one of these in them."

"Grand trees. They give energy to all the others." Elizabeth stopped at my side. She looked at the tree alongside me. "I went to see Thomas. He thinks Rain misses you, Jeth."

My mouth went dry. "I know."

She sighed. "Are you still looking for Shelly?"

"I haven't made any progress, so far."

Elizabeth put her hand on my arm. "Let me help you, Jeth. Together, we might have better luck."

I raised my eyebrows. "I didn't expect you to want to help."

"Look, this is big." She leaned closer to me and dropped her voice. "Cleans can be restored, Jeth. We have to prove it can be permanent, and this is the best way we have."

The tree swayed with another gust. Elizabeth wrapped her arms around herself and shivered. I turned toward her. "Alright. Any ideas where we should look? The banks have been useless so far."

"We'd need to break into security memories if we want to know what they know," she said.

"Liz, those memories are protected. And not by lightweight aeons, either."

"Then it's a good thing both of us are skilled memeotects."

"You want to infiltrate their banks?"

"I don't want to." She looked up at my face. A few strands of hair fluttered at the sides of her face. "We just don't have much choice."

I thought of Ryan again. I hadn't been able to reach him by network lately. As an analyst, he had access to the kind of banks I needed when on the job. "I have an idea, Liz. You remember Ryan Carter, right?"

A pair of cleans approached the tree, crossing a circle carved around the base, which humans were prohibited from passing.

Elizabeth frowned. "The little security guy?"

"He's been out of contact with me for a while. Could be he's working on something secret."

"Something like a hunt for a rogue star?"

I nodded. "It fits his job description."

"Great. Well, how do we find him?"

The cleans began to climb the tree, shimmying up the side to the lowest branches. I envied the athleticism, but at least I still had my mind. They each bore small clippers and climbed along the branch they reached, looking with a bizarre sense of purpose for malformed outgrowths. One of the cleans clipped off a small branch and let it fall to the ground.

I turned to Elizabeth. "We'll work together," I said. Then I reached out with my mind and forwarded all the information I had about Ryan's work to Elizabeth. She accepted the packet of memories and sent me a packet of her own about security forces and analysis teams. Both of us withdrew into our bodily senses for a moment. She smiled at me, eyes shining. Then we dove back into the mental world together.

UNREGISTERED MEMORY, Ryan Carter, Network Security Center, Delta Complex

Ryan hunched forward at the table, face hanging over a plate of vegetable debris and a burger on a bun. His eyes burned after another twelve straight hours of searching the memory banks for clues as to Yashelia's precise location. He already felt as though he had learned too much. Of course, that changed nothing except for the increased risks of punishment if he failed to deliver. The fat sensocycler, Conner Kohl, sat beside Ryan, quietly eating some kind of pie off a tray and visibly savoring every bite with his enhanced sense of taste.

The woman, Commander De Vries, had said they could order anything within reason from outside and someone would bring it to them. Apparently, Kohl had earned his heavy gut. Ryan sighed as he picked up the burger. Kohl might be ridiculous, but he got the job done. Even though Ryan was exhausted, he admitted that much.

In spite of Kohl's efficiency and professionalism on the job, Ryan had not uncovered Yashelia's location yet. Even so, he had it narrowed to one of two parks located south of Lotdel Tower, one that looked unoccupied by a canal, and another in an immense greenhouse run by an enigmatic aeon. Ryan's suspicions told him the greenhouse was a dud place to look. The memory banks held enough information on the aeon owner that Ryan could infer she was innocent.

No, it's got to be that unoccupied park by the canal. Visuals logged by multiple civilian and professional witnesses from as recently as a ten days ago showed glimpses of green deep inside. And green this time of year meant an aeon's garden. Traffic on the water was more limited as a source, but a clean market was nearby. A market like that attracted a lot of people. Ryan figured that's why the reports had been so insistent.

But ten days ago, all information surrounding the abandoned park simply ceased coming in. *I've got you now,* Ryan thought as he finished his burger. They needed to get back in there. Reinvigorated by the food despite the shadows under his eyes, Ryan turned to Conner Kohl.

"You ready?"

Kohl shrugged. His tray was empty of pie. "When you are."

Ryan grinned. "I have a hunch this hunt is almost over." He took a small cup of pure ichor from the table, looked around at the four childlike bodies of the banks in the corners of the room, and then slammed the drink in one swallow. Sweetness exploded in his mouth. Light from the veins in the ceiling clawed at his eyes with raw intensity. Ryan tasted tiny traces of burger and bun on his tongue. His grin widened.

Kohl sipped his own ichor. His eyes grew cold. The red of his hair looked more shocking, and he smelled acutely of lemons, like the pie he had just devoured. Kohl turned to Ryan.

Ryan felt a bit of drool run over his lips. "Let's do this." He set one hand down on the table. Khol put a soft palm over top. Person to person interface was a technique of sensocycling only the best could achieve. Kohl reached out with his sharpened senses and Ryan closed his eyes and went with him, overlaying a view of the physical world like a ghost onto the mental.

Among towers and canals and streets rose mountains of memories and dipped deep canyons of thought. The shapes of humans moved through these obstacles without heed. Ryan could have laughed. He sped through the eyes of humans, birds, and animals, processing views from all angles as he approached the park by the canal. The combination of sensory and memetic skills made for the wildest ride Ryan had ever experienced.

He sensed a mind amid the trees of the park, where the grass and bushes were overgrown. *Someone forgot this place a long time ago.* He rode the mind of a squirrel along the branch. The jittery creature got him close enough to jump skyward to a bird on its way south. From there, Ryan looked down. A towering gray-barked tree with vibrant green leaves stood within the overgrown center of the park, bent over with the weight of the limbs on one side.

The heart of a forest. Shapes moved around the tree, desperately hacking and sawing at branches with crude metal tools. Ryan sensed no information in those minds. *Cleans, huh?* He searched for the spark, the spark of an aeon's mind, and he found it near the base of the tree.

"There. You. Are!" Ryan laughed with triumph and nearly fell out of his chair as he opened his eyes. He hung onto the back of the seat with one arm. "You saw that, too? You got that, right?"

Kohl nodded, a smile on his face.

Ryan laughed again. "Jackpot, baby! Store it in the banks. I'll call the commander."

Kohl removed his hand from Ryan's, and then closed his eyes again. Ryan snickered as he stood up and focused his mind on the commander.

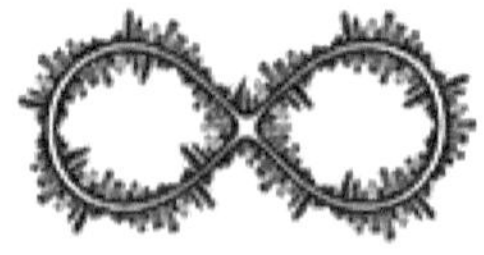

ELIZABETH AND I PLUNGED through the cityscape, two minds together. Without a skilled sensor, neither of us could accurately sense the physical world, but the minds of people gleamed and hummed and seared in the mental world. I searched for Ryan Carter's mind.

A smell of ozone burned some ten or fifteen kilometers to the north, intense but distant. I recognized the smell as the one Ryan's mind carried with it in the mental world, and was thankful despite the bitter twinge in my nose. The fingers of my mind reached out and found Elizabeth's projection. I guided her in the direction I had caught a whiff of Ryan. What looked like a dark cloud billowed over a cluster of bright minds.

Wherever Ryan was, he was surrounded by people with powerful barriers and quick emotional antibodies. I could tell the defenses by the phantom signals that danced on the outside of their signature sounds and shapes, colors and feelings. A bright flash flickered at the center of the black clouds, a solitary bolt of jagged lightning. I guessed that pointed toward Ryan.

He got intense when he worked evidently, but it finally explained his odd projection signature. When lightning strikes in the real world, ozone in the air burns. Ryan took that concept to his personal mental space.

The sensation of my projected consciousness racing over a tableau of bright bank towers and the diverse minds of others infused in me a sense of power as Elizabeth and I glided down into the clouds that surrounded Ryan's lightning. My mind glanced off a barrier I had not even glimpsed as I got closer. Elizabeth, slightly behind my projection, skirted the barrier without colliding. My head ached, but I refused to return my mind to my physical body.

I rejoined Elizabeth, and we circled the barrier, wary of the nearby lights and sounds and smells of the minds that occupied the clouds before us. "They're going to be aware of us," I said through our connection.

Her projection flickered against the invisible wall. "Make sure you hide your identity information."

"Right. You too."

We each took a moment to bury our information within ourselves. I picked a memory of pain as intense as I could approach, the one from the hornet bites, and hid my information in the stings. Anyone who tried to uncover that truth would have to endure the same pain I had back then to do so. I hid some of my recent memories in the bee stings as well, the ones about Rebecca and Rain reawakening. Particular memories were harder to smoke out of a mind, but with enough mental attackers, details could be uncovered.

I rejoined Elizabeth at the barrier. "Any ideas how to get through?"

Her frosted mind turned slowly before the invisible wall. Tendrils of consciousness extended and felt carefully along the barrier. I watched as she appraised the defenses, then set to evaluating it for myself. Clearing a barrier could take some time. Our bodies were still in Bailey Court Garden and, for a moment, I worried about being found out. I suppressed the feeling, burying it under a thin layer of thought about my mission, about Rebecca.

My mind brushed against the barrier. The wall was painful to the touch and appeared to enclose the dark clouds completely. I withdrew my mental fingers. *There's always a chink in the armor or I wouldn't be able to sense beyond this wall.* I probed a few points. This was no simple mental maze. A barrier like this had to be created by multiple minds at once.

"Any idea where the anchors for this might be?" I asked. "Or how many there are?"

Elizabeth withdrew her tendrils from the barrier. "There has to be at least three of them. As to where they are, I'm not sure."

Anchors provided the basis for temporary mental structures, whereas banks usually formed more permanent constructs. Disrupting even one of them could cause the barrier to become unstable. I racked my memory for the types of clues I should be looking for. With a barrier this strong, there had to be at least one outside the barrier. Elizabeth must have had a similar thought.

"We should check the perimeter," she said. "This barrier feels curved."

"Split up?" I asked.

"Probably, but signal me if you find an anchor."

"Gotcha."

I circled around the barrier but found nothing on the outside. Oddly, the area around the barrier was only sparsely dotted with minds on the outside. Within, I could sense at least three dozen minds. I checked the identities of all ten of the minds I found on the outside. The pair that made me the most suspicious turned out to be a mother with a child in a stroller. I continued circling, but when I reached the far side of the barrier, Elizabeth had yet to arrive.

Nervous tension crept into my mind. I sent a packet to Elizabeth, just to make sure she wasn't in trouble. She fired one back. *I've found the anchor.*

Charged with even more nerves, I put on a burst of speed and sailed over the top of the barrier, estimating it to be spherical. I was lucky enough to be right, and I sensed Elizabeth's mind below me, near the edge of the barrier. Then I plunged down to float beside her.

A single mind huddled near a bank-formed memory tower a short distance from the tower.

"That's him." Elizabeth floated toward the tower. "We'll have to attack if we want to disrupt the barrier."

"But they've got enough minds inside, we'll have to fight if they notice a breach."

"I'm not up for tangling with forty military consciousnesses."

"Neither am I," I said, "but we've got to do something."

"You're the faster thinker. I'll disrupt the anchor. You get in and get the information."

That worried me a little. If I darted inside fast enough, I could get to Ryan before they caught me, but Ryan's mind would not be undefended, between his memetic and security training. He might be tougher than me defense-wise.

"I'll try," I said, "but I might not get all the way out, so once you break the barrier, get out of here."

She hesitated for a moment, and I could imagine her frown of concern. "Alright." She flew toward the anchor.

I waited for what seemed like an hour, primed to rush inside, and burning with nerves. The barrier before me flickered, visible in blue haze for a moment. Then it broke into splinters, and the shards rained down around the clouds. I accelerated into the storm.

A trio of minds noticed me. I evaded one of them completely through sheer speed. Another moved to block my path. I dodged that one, too, but hit the third moving sideways. The mind identified herself as Alesia De Vries, commander of a purifier unit under Sudhatho. That made sense.

Her mental maze was dense with turns and dead ends. My swift pace allowed me to backtrack as quickly as I was cut off. A flame burst up in front of me, blocking my path suddenly. I hesitated only for a moment, then dove though. Fiery pain burned through my mind and I gasped, almost thrown back to my body by the agony. Then I emerged from the fire, seared through with misery but within De Vries' mind.

She sent a team of antibodies after me. As I looked up through my dazed and teary mental eyes I glimpsed a though moving within her mind. It looked like a file cabinet with three words written on its side. *Rogue Star, Yashelia.*

She is the commander, I thought. *If they've found Yashelia, she should know.*

De Vries' antibodies swarmed around me, pounding at the edges of my psyche. One of them injected a cleaning agent into my unconscious, the kind that would clear all my barriers in no time. I leapt for the thought cabinet above me, tearing it out of the grip of each antibody one by one. Only the injector remained embedded. I reached out and seized the cabinet.

In real time, it took only seconds to capture the information, but here it would feel far longer. I held on tight as the antibodies closed in once again. Heavy blows rained down upon me, battering my projected essence to the core. I held on.

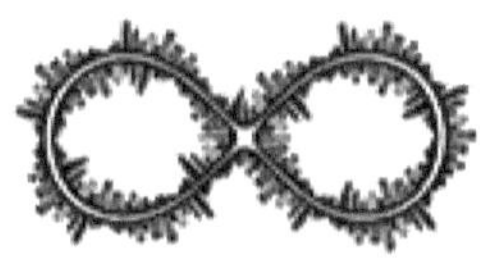

9

I FELT AS THOUGH I was falling through shadows. Pain flared behind my eyes. Blood rushed through my head and pounded against the inside of my temples. I felt my brows furrow, and then my eyes flew open. Light stabbed into my eyes from the window in my bedroom. I lay atop the covers and listened to my breath slow from the panicked draw in and push out.

The pain did not subside and throbbed in my skull even worse. I grunted, drawing the attention of Elizabeth who I became aware of as she turned toward me from my doorway. She sighed, sounding relieved, and walked over to my side.

"How do you feel?" she asked.

I squeezed my eyes shut. "Not the best."

She tilted her head to the side and looked down at me. "They stopped you pretty hard."

Despite the ache in my skull, I smiled. "I got it."

She frowned. "You found the information?"

I winced as I sat up. "Yeah," I said. "Shelly's at the overgrown park near the clean market, but on our side of the canal."

Elizabeth nodded, and looked ready to reply, but the sound of footsteps from behind stopped her.

Thomas walked in. "Hey, man," he said. "Are you alright?"

"I'll live," I said. "We have to hurry."

"I got some things from my associates ready. They're interested to see if we can find proof that aeons can restore cleans." Thomas leaned against the door frame. "Where are we going?"

"The park southwest of here, beside the canal." I swung my legs off the bed with a groan of effort.

Elizabeth stepped back from my bed and folded her arms. "You want to fight an aeon?"

Thomas rubbed his goatee. "Yeah, Shelly's not just gonna give us her blood."

I fell to my knees beside the bed, then rummaged underneath until I pulled out the shotgun box I had hidden there, along with a case of shells. I supported myself on the wall and stood, then turned around.

Elizabeth shook her head. Her eyes fell from my face to the weapon. "Even if that can hurt her, what then?"

"I've got this," said Thomas. "I have some hypos upstairs. Should be able to get a lot of blood out that way."

"Good." I massaged my temples with one hand. The pain began to fade from that spot little by little, but remained in the back of my head just as intense as ever. "Sudhatho was sending a strike force to attack the place. How long was I out?"

"Half an hour," Elizabeth said. "Thomas helped me carry you up here." She handed my keys to me. "I let us all in."

I looked into her eyes. "Thanks. It's a good thing I didn't try that solo."

"You're a big guy," Thomas said. "I'd rather not have to do that again."

I couldn't help but smirk. "I don't plan to make a habit of getting knocked into my own subconscious."

"So," Elizabeth said, "what's the plan? You two go to this garden. Get Yashelia's blood and run back here without security noticing you? Any sensor they have could flag you with a round trip that long."

"We'll need someone to run interference for us then," I said. "Are you up for it, Liz?"

She took a deep breath, eyes locked with mine. "I'll do what I can."

I put a hand on her shoulder. "I owe you one."

"What about Rain?" Thomas asked. "She's still up in the Mangrove Suite. If something happens I don't think we should leave her alone."

"I'll watch her," Elizabeth said. "Don't worry about it."

Thomas raised an eyebrow. Elizabeth rolled her eyes. "Don't imagine things," she said.

"Can't help it."

I rubbed the back of my skull. "Thomas, the train can get us close, but we might need a getaway plan."

"My van," said Thomas. He glanced at Elizabeth. "You ever drive?"

"I grew up around trucks," she said. "I can handle it."

The memory of the little girl who looked like Elizabeth crying at the front of the auto repair place returned to my mind. I took my hand from Elizabeth's shoulder. "Couldn't do this without you," I said.

She flushed in the midst of an attempt at a shrug. "I want to know the truth, too," she said. "Partner."

I nodded to her, then turned to Thomas, leaning on the stock of my shotgun like a crutch. "Let's move." I winced. "But first, get me some painkillers. Damn, my skull hurts."

UNREGISTERED MEMORY, Ryan Carter, Network Security Center, Delta Complex

Sudhatho's strike force rolled out of Delta Complex an hour after the security breach Commander De Vries had been involved in. Ryan watched the four armored trucks from the window of a boardroom in the office building where had had been stationed. Conner Kohl sat at a table in the same room, digging into another slice of pie, pecan this time. Past Kohl, by the door, stood Commander De Vries with her arms folded and her head down.

She had removed her armor and masked helmet, revealing a surprisingly young face. Her blonde hair was tied back in a short ponytail, which shook as she seethed quietly. The officer in charge of the complex had not liked her leaking the information Ryan and Kohl had uncovered. Evidently they blamed De Vries and had detained her and her hires to minimize any other possible memory spillage.

Ryan had to credit Sudhatho's security forces, they took precautions fast. Evidently, when De Vries tangled with the mentality that had broken through the barrier, the still-unidentified invader had gotten a glimpse into her mind. She had given up the plan, so if the rogue star was behind the attack it would only be a matter of time before they got the wheels turning to prepare defenses. Ryan turned from the window to where the red-haired Kohl sat eating calmly.

"How long until they release us?" Ryan asked.

Kohl kept eating with an expression of glee on his face.

De Vries turned toward Ryan. Her blue eyes flashed. "Once they've run the operation, they'll investigate us. If we're lucky we won't lose our jobs." She clenched one fist at her side.

"You believe that?" Ryan asked. "Then why are you so angry?"

"This would have been my first chance at a Rogue Star." De Vries wrinkled her nose. "I guess I hired the right analysts for the mission. You two found her, but they don't trust you either."

"We're intelligence assets," Ryan said. "Can't have us wandering off during the op."

Below them engines fired, drawing Ryan's attention back to them. Armored cars rolled out of the complex. In the distance the shape of Sudhatho's light ship hung over the city, as it turned slowly toward the south. This particular security force appeared to have a mad on for Yashelia. Most rogue stars wouldn't draw a great aeon like Sudhatho into battle.

Ryan turned to Kohl and De Vries as the last of the cars left through the gate. "Looks like they'll be fighting soon."

Kohl took a bite of his pie, a look of relish on his face. De Vries stalked from the door to the table where Kohl sat. She sat down at a chair beside him and looked toward Ryan. "Is there something you want to do?"

Ryan glanced at Kohl. "I want to watch."

Kohl finished the pie and glanced at Ryan. "I'm game, you have ichor?"

Ryan frowned. "There's the problem," he said. "I've only got traces left after our big find."

Kohl smiled. "I'm covered. The last pie was made with ichor."

De Vries folded her arms and leaned back. "If you fill me in on what you see, I won't tell anyone."

"Deal," said Ryan. He walked to the table and sat down on Kohl's other side. "Let's do this."

In seconds, Ryan's mind went blazing across the city, free to search, and watch, and see once more.

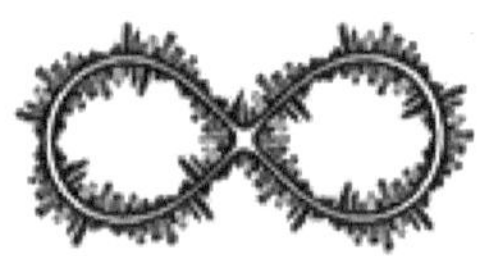

THE TRAIN CARRIED THOMAS and I south in an otherwise empty passenger car. When we reached the station closest to the park where the security forces had located Yashelia, we disembarked and went on foot through windswept streets. I carried the shotgun in a long ski case to avoid drawing attention to it. Thomas hid a small handgun in his coat. I also had my flask of ichor and an empty hypo for Yashelia's blood.

I couldn't help but wonder how much ichor we would have to take from her, to restore Rebecca permanently. It might not be possible at all. I pushed that thought away.

The park loomed before us. The trees on the outside lost orange leaves every now and then to gusts of wind. I stared at the tree line and the dead grass at the base of each trunk. The hand that held the case with the shotgun shook. Yashelia, aeon, rogue star, it didn't matter what she was. She packed enough power Thomas and I wouldn't stand a chance in a straight battle.

"We need to sneak up on her," I said. "Hell if I know how we can, though."

A packet pinged me from Elizabeth. I accessed it immediately.

"I can't sense any minds in that park. Must be just Yashelia because she's invisible over the network."

I sent back, *"She has some cleans in there with her too. They're always mentally invisible as well."*

Thomas and I stopped at the corner of the last building before the park. Elizabeth's next packet arrived as I peered around the wall at the trees, seeking movement.

"I've architected a few poison packets. I'll do my best to hit anybody you see with them."

I frowned as Thomas removed the pistol from his coat's inside pocket. After a moment of hesitation, I replied to Elizabeth.

"Good, but cleans and aeons probably won't stop from that."

"I can at least distract them," she sent back.

"True." I turned to Thomas. "Stay sharp." I set the case on the sidewalk, looked down the empty street over my shoulder, and then cracked it open. The shotgun barrel gleamed dully under the cloudy sky. I hefted the weapon, then loaded it. The weapon could hold eight shells.

I only had six, but I loaded them up as carefully as my unpracticed hands could manage. "Alright, Shelly, ready or not."

Thomas glanced at me, hunched forward a little, both hands on the grip of his pistol.

"You ready to kick a hornet's nest?" I asked.

He shrugged and then straightened. "I'm ready to find out what's inside this one."

I nudged the case I had brought the shotgun in to one side. As I stepped past the box, a mental alarm went off in my head, the voice of an aeon local to this part of the city.

"Citizens, security is performing an operation in Lind Park this afternoon and possibly into the evening hours. Be advised the area is very dangerous. Do not enter," the voice said in my mind.

I put a palm to my temple, felt it throb, and then lowered my hand. Thomas glanced at me. I shook my head. "Let's go."

We hustled across the street, heads down, weapons held close. My head began to ache despite the painkillers I had taken before leaving Lotdel Tower. Thomas and I reached the tree line and sheltered behind large bushes on either side of a path through a tangled thicket. Thomas checked the corner, then motioned for me to follow him.

The two of us met up on the path.

"Have you been in security?" I asked.

"I washed out after a month," said Thomas, "but I remember a little."

The edges of the path were blocked by dense undergrowth. We walked down the center, cautious, moving slow. I didn't see anything, so I turned to Thomas in the shadows of the tall trees where we stood.

Thomas pointed through the gloom ahead of us, and I glimpsed movement, a faint sign of human life in the shadows beyond the path. "Do you see that?" he asked.

"Yeah." My breath became a faint mist before me. "Can you tell if its human?"

He laid the barrel of his pistol across his shoulder and squinted ahead. "Not yet."

I took a step forward down the path. It suddenly seemed narrower, and the leaves louder underfoot. I raised the shotgun and kept moving, conscious of the rustling in the branches and the crackle of my footsteps in dead and fallen foliage. Thomas followed me. I glanced back and saw him take the pistol grip in both hands again. I clutched the shotgun tighter and pressed on.

About forty meters from an opening in the path ahead, a twig snapped beneath my foot and at the same moment another sound, a high-pitched giggle, came from my right. I spun and looked for the owner of the voice. Yashelia had to be around here somewhere, and whatever had set her at odds with the rest of the aeons, I supposed had also damaged her mind.

"Thomas?" I stared into the woods of the park.

No answer.

I glanced behind me, where Thomas had been just a second before. He was gone. My eyes widened, and I checked my other sides. I found no trace except for a slight whiff of bitterness in the air. I gulped and held tight to my shotgun as if it could protect me from a rogue star or aeon. What had I been thinking?

How had he just vanished? I reached out over the network, searching for any sign of Thomas in the park or near it, but I found nothing. My mentality felt a bit unfocused, probably from my headache, but a human mind is an obvious element. One doesn't just lose a friend on the network. Given the right amount of ichor one could even reach to the western megalopolis and communicate directly.

"Thomas?" I hissed. "Thomas, where are you?"

I waited. No answer. Wind played with the branches overhead, and they creaked against the reddening sky. I turned and looked down the path leading into the park. Then I raised my shotgun and started forward.

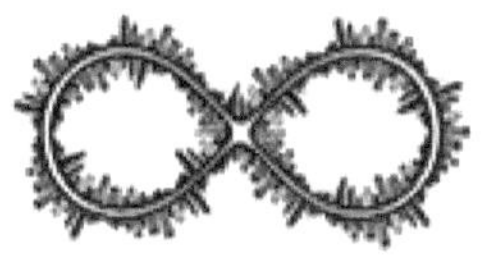

10

UNREGISTERED MEMORY, Elizabeth Ashwood, The Mangrove Suite, Lotdel Tower

"You lost track of him?" Elizabeth said over direct connection to Thomas. She had to block out all her senses to communicate in real time with him, but she knew she was trembling.

"He was there one minute and gone the next," Thomas said. *"I didn't notice anything off before that."*

"Where are you now?" she asked.

"Still on the path where I lost him."

She felt herself intake breath as her concentration frayed. *"You didn't lose him. Keep looking."*

"Look, I don't see him. I consider that lost."

"Consider it whatever you want. Just find him."

His mind flared up, probably with a potential retort, but then subsided. *"I'll try."*

"Send me a message when you find him. I'll scan the network for him."

"Got it."

Elizabeth disconnected for a moment, smelled the perfume of the room where she stood. The clean woman, Rain, sat on the bed looking at her with empty eyes. Elizabeth shuddered at the thought of her there the whole time Elizabeth sacrificed her external senses for the network. She hadn't moved at all since Elizabeth told her to sit down. At least cleans obeyed, usually. Elizabeth began to pace back and forth, one hand on her forehead. *Where did you go, Jeth? How does someone just vanish like that?*

Her mind hit on one possibility. Sensotecture. Like memetics, sensory networking could be used as an attack, and when it was someone could feed an illusion into the mind of someone whose security they breached. Thomas could be standing right beside Jeth and not see him, and that could even go both ways if they were attacked simultaneously. Sensory hedges could be used to block spying and keep privacy during important assemblies. The only problem with that theory was the need for multiple sensotects to pull off the attack.

And Elizabeth had not detected even one other mind in the forest before Thomas and Jeth had gone in. She groaned with frustration and turned to Rain and grimaced. "Great, stuck in a room with someone mindless. Think Elizabeth. There has to be some way to help them find each other."

Rain looked up at Elizabeth, eyes vacant, then reached to the table at the head of the bed and picked up a vial of ichor kept there for customers. Probably so they enjoy their time here better. Elizabeth's grimace turned into a scowl. "What is that supposed to do?" she asked. "I'm already above normal dose."

The clean woman shook her head. "Not for you. For me."

Elizabeth took a step back from Rain, eyes widening slightly in shock. "What good will that do? Do you remember training as a sensocycler?"

Rain shook her head. "Words aren't easy."

"Right, you can barely talk." Elizabeth took a deep breath. "Look, I don't know what kind of training you had as a person, but you're a clean. You don't know enough to do any of that stuff, and you won't ever again unless we get you Yashelia's blood."

"Don't be mad."

"I'm not mad." Elizbeth folded her arms. "I'm worried. I need a solution."

Rain held out the vial to her. "Let me try."

"Fine. Drink it. If you're all the way clean, it won't change anything."

Rain nodded. "I know." She raised the vial to her lips. Elizabeth glowered at her as the amber liquid held within the glass drained into Rain's mouth. The dark woman blinked her eyes, then squeezed them tightly shut. "Take my hands." She held her palms out to Elizabeth.

With a sigh, Elizabeth pressed her palms to Rain's, then wrapped her fingers around to hold on. She closed her eyes. She extended her senses into the network and found more than the mountains and canyons of data and memory, but also a cityscape stretching in every direction for as far as her mentality could see. Beside her projection, a faint sensation of warmth radiated from in front of her where Rain sat in the Mangrove Suite, a mind, however subtle.

She never faded completely. She's been here all along, and I couldn't tell.

Rain's warmth reached out and enveloped Elizabeth's mind. A wave of intense pleasure ran through her thoughts, accompanied by memories of home before the accident, of her sister, of Jeth. Elizabeth fought to keep her knees from buckling and held herself up.

"Let's go," said a gentle voice from mind to mind.

Elizabeth pulsed back affirmation in her own cold way. She reached out with her mind, aided by Rain's senses, and flew across the city into the eyes of Thomas in the forested park where flickers of shapes moving on a different path visible through the trees caught her eye. With no sign visible of Jeth, she leapt into one of the minds on the far path and listened for anything within.

Other purifiers moved in behind the man she listened from on the path. They rustled leaves and passed orders down the line in hushed voices. A single crow circled over them. Elizabeth only barely noticed the bird before she was looking through the animal's eyes. The crow caught a cool draft of air and rode it out over the center of the park where a massive gray tree with thorns on its branches leaned to one side, looking almost like a person doubled over due to the weight of overgrown branches on one side.

At the foot of the tree stood a figure, a man whose mind seemed somehow distant. She tried to reach out to him but could not get a grip. The man gripped a shotgun and stared up at the tree from below with clouded, sightless eyes. *Jeth.*

Elizabeth sent her mind flying back to Thomas. She dropped a packet for him at his mental doorstep, telling him where to find Jeth. She hastily added they were both under illusions and to be careful of sensotects in the park. He sent only a hasty reply, confirming he understood. Then he pressed forward into the forest, Elizabeth's senses along for the ride.

IN THE SHADOW OF A tree over fifteen meters tall even when bent on its side, after minutes of creeping through the forest tensed, I reevaluated my sense of the situation. I had seen no one else so far, but whatever had made Thomas disappear could be dangerous, and I knew Yashelia was in the park somewhere. My ears picked up the sound of soft footsteps moving leaves to my left. I turned and looked down that path.

Black armored troops moved in the shadows on the path, rifles at the ready. I ducked behind the trunk of the massive tree that resembled a hunched and thorny version of the one in Bailey Court Garden. My heart thumped in my chest, and I hoped the security forces hadn't seen me.

I reached out with my mind and found no others in range. Evidently someone had found a way to disrupt my network connection, because I knew what I saw. Those purifiers looked real as anything, but if I was caught in an illusion they could appear anywhere to drive me in the direction the puppeteer wanted. *Step one has to be breaking the illusion.*

My back to the tree, I took a deep breath, and then delved into the haze of my mind. I let my instinct guide me down paths of light that distinguished between old memories and current feelings.

I felt as though I descended through mist. A downward tug pulled at the pit of my stomach, and my view inhibited by branches and interconnected sinewy fibers of unconscious understanding. I felt as though I was in the depths of a swamp, surrounded by trees and fog, knee deep in muddy water.

Discolored liquid lapped at the edges of my perspective, and a bitter tang filled my nose. I recognized the memory from the Green Valley, spring when the river overflowed its bank and filled the lowlands. Trees could drown in such deep water, but many had adapted to survive the season long ago. The whole scene was frozen, birds in flight silenced by the snapshot. If my brother was here, he could tell me the names of each species of insect and animal.

But Luke wasn't here. Luke had never been to the east where I lived. Where I stood in a park, not in a swamp. Why had I imagined my body in the memory? The mud on which I stood sucked down into shadow. My bare feet sank deeper in. This wasn't how I had felt back then. I hadn't stood paralyzed and sinking.

What had I done? I pulled myself out of there. The thought got me pulling on my legs, but it did not free me. I grabbed a tree branch and hung on to the arm of the illusory tree. Yet the pull of the mud grew stronger, and gravity felt heavier. The force weighed on me unnaturally. I gasped in pain. This wasn't just my mind. This was part of the illusion.

I hadn't even noticed my defenses getting breached. Who could have brought this memory out? It had only been a moment in reality, yet here I struggled not to sink. A giggle echoed in my ears from across the mire. I glanced up from the brackish water and found Yashelia standing on a tree branch across a clearing dressed as I remembered her from the Mangrove Suite. Pale hair streamed out over the swamp, carried by a silent breeze.

"Rebecca had similar memories, filthy things that they are," she said, "but soon you will both be clean of them."

I glared at her, grip slipping on the branch where I clung for the survival of not just my mind, but for Rebecca's. Beside Yashelia another form materialized, a small woman looking as if she had simply stepped out of the air. She looked hazy and her clothes and face were indistinct, probably because I had never met her and my mind only rendered the vaguest shape.

"Mistress," said the woman, "the purifiers are close to the tree."

"Delay them." The wound over Yashelia's eye dripped ichor which ran down her face, and then fell into the water below her. "This man must be cleaned."

I grimaced. "Why are you doing this?" I said. "Why did you want Rain?"

"Your memories will be gone in a moment if you let go." Yashelia smiled. "Be a good little boy and you need never know."

I gritted my teeth. "But I want to know, and I'm not letting go until I do."

"Mistress," said the hazy woman beside Yashelia, "we should hurry."

Yashelia's eyes moved to the woman at her side. "Leave this to me. Confuse the troops."

"As you wish." The woman faded completely back into the mist. Part of my mentality, the part that wasn't stuck in a swamp of floodwaters, could still sense a faint presence of her nearby.

Yashelia turned back to me. "Are you prepared to become clean?"

I spat into the water between us.

Her face pinched. Unnatural aeonic beauty warped into a ghoulish mask, and she glared at me. Then she was on a branch above me, hands reaching out to pry my fingers from where I hung on. Her hand wrapped around my wrist, then jerked on my arm. My palm tore and became bloody, and I fell into the water and mud of the flooded forest floor with a yelp.

I struggled on the surface, fighting for air. A cogent thought arose from fear. *Is this how it feels to be cleaned?* Yashelia reached toward me and drove my head into the abyssal waters of the swamp.

Colorless light spilled into my eyes even as oblivion claimed the memory of the forest. Thoughts seemed far off. Someone called to me, a woman, her voice distant and sharp. I fought through a storm of bright colors like binding strings that then tore and seeped away into light. The voice remained, though I could not understand her. My own language sounded foreign in my echoing head.

Then I was no longer a body. I was a mind alone, free of the memory the illusionist had imprisoned me within. My projected mentality returned in its willowy, shifting state, my familiar presence on the network. I fought to open my eyes, to break the connection. I thought about a nest of hornets, my brother's face, a van on a road, a girl in a shawl, a woman dancing on a stage in a marketplace. *These are the things I'm going to lose. The cleaning isn't over yet.*

The voice bit into my mind, lodging in my everything.

"Elizabeth, is that you??"

"It's me. And Rain."

"You found me. I guess that means I can say goodbye."

Elizabeth sounded insistent. *"Jeth, she's not touching you anymore."*

A second voice cut in, a familiar one but with a soft tone. *"Rebecca you always made a good sensocycler."*

"Jeth, open your eyes."

I pulled back from my memories. My eyes flew open. I stood beside the tree as I had before, but with a set of footprints in the leaves beside me, then leading off under the overhanging tree. I looked around the side of the tree.

Ahead of me in that direction the park burned. Bright orange flames licked tree trunks and ignited fallen leaves. Here and there, purifiers in dark armor sprinted. Gunfire howled through the forest. Mentally, I felt Elizabeth and Rain were close, probably watching through my eyes right now. The spell must have broken. *Where is Yashelia? Those footsteps must have been hers, but where is she now?*

My head pounded with an illusion hangover. I pressed my palm to the trunk of the great hunched tree to steady myself, cutting my finger on thorny growth from its side. Blood trickled down to my palm, but I was past caring.

I closed my eyes and took a deep breath. My network connection reactivated. I confirmed the presence of Elizabeth and Rain in my mind and decided I'd have to wait to ask how Elizabeth had accessed Rebecca's skills with her cleaned. To my left, where the tree stood, sank a great pit, walled with golden and glowing memory that flickered and flashed, a mind at my fingertips.

I felt the mind within the tree, an enormous mind, one several times larger and more expansive than any I'd ever felt before. *"It's a mystery where the thoughts of aeons come from,"* said Elizabeth in my head. *"Don't be too hasty."*

"What else could it be? This tree, it contains a mind."

"I sense it, through you," she said, *"but be careful. A mind is a dangerous place."*

"But if there's any truth to finding Rebecca's memories, I have to try and do something. Now. While I have the chance."

Before she could reply I walked to the edge of the great pit of memories, and leapt into the tree's mind.

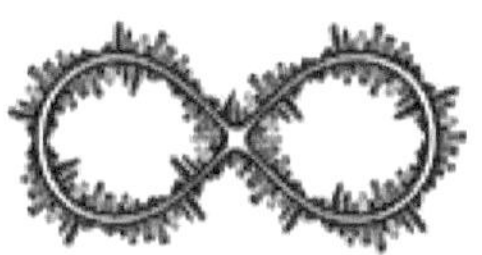

I FELL INTO THE MIND, projection plummeting past glowing banks of memories. A barrier of shimmering transparent matter raced toward me, to block my descent, but I armored myself in determination. I hit the barrier and it shattered. It tore at me, saddened me with an external emotion, and slowed my movement. More transparent, shining barriers raced to intercept me from all along the tunnel. Two overhead blocked the exit.

They surrounded me completely about midway down the pit, then began to close in. Active barriers like this are tricky, and with my determination momentum lost, I had little chance to break them. Still, I lashed out with an arm like a whip. My blow rebounded from the barrier, leaving me with a shadow's flicker of despair from Yashelia's own mentality. Below me, green disks gathered in the pit. I suspected they were antibodies, but they looked so sickly and morose I doubted they would simply repel me if I let them connect.

Antibodies could contain emotions, and if the despair I felt from my blows against the barriers was any indication, Yashelia tried to sap the willpower and joy of anyone who entered her mind. The green disks ascended, floating leeches ready to bleed my mind dry. And there, I floated, already imprisoned by mental barriers.

As the antibodies drew closer a high-pitched squeal reached my ears ahead of them. I struggled against the barriers around me, mind throbbing with pain coupled with irritation added by the sound I realized must be a sensory barrier. It quickly began to disrupt my own thoughts. No sooner would I have one, then the whine pierced deeper and drove it from my attention. Antibodies pulsed in shades of sickening green all around my barrier cage.

My efforts to break out seemed useless, and if I escaped, the antibodies would surely attack immediately. If I weakened my resolve in breaking out they might easily defeat me on the outside. Already, my thoughts were slower, and the inhibiting tone whining through my being could not be denied. With what little concentration I had, I peered through the transparent barriers, looking up and down the memories stacked all the way up the walls of the pit.

Not one of these memory banks looked large enough to hold a human mentality, so if Rebecca was here, I would not find her within any of them. I peered down, sharpening my senses and focusing all my attention on the depths. Some distance below, the pit opened into a glowing cavern of network information. *That could be it. She must keep memories there, and when she needs them, her ichor carries them through her body. This could be why aeons can't be detected on the network unless they choose to be. Their minds are protected in these trees.*

Antibodies closed in on my cage. The barriers hemming me in from above parted to allow an antibody that had passed overhead to descend into my prison. I darted upward, but not fast enough to get my entire mentality free of the cage. The two barriers slammed on either side of me. I screamed in agony, racked with guilt and sorrow from sources outside myself. All that pain pressed in on me from both sides. Stricken by grief that I somehow knew I had caused myself, I almost sank back into the cage. Only one persistent thought allowed me to keep fighting.

These feelings aren't mine. I slipped free of the barriers looped around them, dodging swarms of antibodies as I went.

I hoped my hunch to dive deeper was correct as I flew into the cavern. Memories played like moving paintings on the walls, images of lives and places I had never seen, the faces of men and women known by those who had been cleaned by Yashelia.

Dozens of humanoid projections flickered before my mind's eye, each one distinct but composed of many incongruous features. Scents of perfume and cooking meat and sewage warred with my senses. An uproar of chaotic sounds and voices filled my ears as I plunged deeper into the chamber. I reached out and felt the soft and stiff, the cold and warm with the fingertips of my mind. At last, I tasted a kiss on my lips, and this one sensation alone was familiar to me.

This sensation belonged in not one memory within the tree, but in two. I had only kissed Rebecca once when I'd known her, and the taste of her fled through the shifting projections and gleaming antibodies. I chased the feeling. Antibodies brushed my consciousness, and I repelled them as quickly as I could, flinging them toward the roof of the cavern with dread building in my stomach every time I touched one.

I raced after Rebecca's kiss, my first kiss. A yawning gulf of morning light stretched out below me. An opening in the cavern revealed treetops far below, burning with a fresh dawn. The kiss led me into that forest once more. And then I felt myself inside my body, but not the body I had grown accustomed to over years of plenty and years of building thoughts for others.

The body I inhabited was young and excited and pulsing with hormones. I stood in the morning of the Green Valley in autumn, cold light and misty air. Disoriented, my mind did not control the actions of this body. The past me turned and looked up the hill to a house with a roman columned porch and a white door, the house Rebecca's family had moved into after a year of living in the Green Valley and finally moving up in status.

I climbed the steps to her door, following the sense of her kiss. I opened the door with a slow turn of the knob to keep it quiet. My feet carried me through the house as quietly as young me could manage, careful not to wake the rest of the family. I made my way to the back door where a broad deck overlooked the backyard and a sharp decline. By the wooden railing of the deck, stood Rebecca.

She turned toward me, shawl over her hair. I walked across the boards of the deck and met her by the side. She smiled at me. "Good morning, Jeth."

The blood of my younger self ran with as much nervousness as excitement. I reached out tentatively. Rebecca took my hand with hers. Her other hand pulled the shawl back from her dark hair. We leaned into each other, then fully embraced. Lips met in light and joy, freedom and truth, the kiss as Rebecca remembered.

I found her.

"You need to come with me," I said from my mind as I watched the scene. "We need to leave."

Her voice spoke in my ear, "I've been lost. Jeth, help me find my way."

I reached into the scene and touched Rebecca's young face. Then I drew back and found her presence following me, not the presence of the teenager, but one of the adult woman she became before being cleaned.

We fled from the dreamed memory, from the cavern, from the pit, from the tree.

I woke, startled and dazed. The forest burned and gunshots cracked through the air. I staggered back from the tree.

"Elizabeth, can you help Rebecca find Rain?"

"I'll lead her."

I stepped back from the tree, still dazed from my deep mind delving. Thunder roared. A massive shadow moved over the clearing, darkening the already cloudy sky except for the flickering light veins that ran along its sides. Sudhatho's light ship hovered above the overgrown park. I stared up at it and trembled.

UNREGISTERED MEMORY, Elizabeth Ashwood, The Mangrove Suite, Lotdel Tower

Elizabeth sat on the floor, leaning against the side of the bed. Her heart hurt, and her breathing came in gasps. The intensity of the mental effort to bring Rebecca's mind back to her body had more than drained her. The effort had hurt her.

The woman lying on the bed, legs dangling over the side past Elizabeth, opened her eyes. Rebecca's breath went in and out steadily. Rebecca slipped off the bed and crouched beside Elizabeth. "Are you alright?" she asked.

Elizabeth gazed up at her face, eyes wide with recognition. "Hello, Rebecca."

A broad smile formed on Rebecca's face. "You brought me here. Thank you."

Elizabeth managed to return to Rebecca's smile weakly. "I did my best."

"It was enough. Can you walk?"

"Maybe," Elizabeth said. *Jeth and Thomas are still in danger.*

"We have to hurry."

Rebecca offered Elizabeth her hand. She took it, and Rebecca helped her up. Elizabeth steadied herself on Rebecca's arm. Her other palm pressed to her forehead. "We're going after them. Aren't we?"

The burden of Rebecca's memories of her time since her small taste of Yashelia's ichor felt like heavy weights in the back of Elizabeth's mind. Everything was so strange.

Rebecca's hand clasped Elizabeth's wrist. "We need to get to the park as fast as we can."

Elizabeth nodded. "Thomas' van," she said. "We need to get it from the parking garage."

Rebecca helped Elizabeth out the door and toward the elevator. Elizabeth reached out with her senses and found Rebecca's mind nearby. She did her best to shroud them from the senses of others but only had rudimentary knowledge of sensotecture. Managing it in real time was almost too much for her. They reached the bottom of the shaft in the parking garage under the tower, and the doors opened. The two of them walked out of the elevator and headed for the van.

Elizabeth took the wheel, not trusting Rebecca to drive so soon after her restoration. *And what about me?* Elizabeth grimaced. *I'll have to do my best.*

Rebecca slammed the passenger door. Elizabeth drove.

11

THE TREES IN THE PARK burned with black smoke while the light ship hung in the air overhead. I clutched the shotgun and crept under the branches of Yashelia's tree and found the armored body of a purifier in the foliage beyond. Blood ran from the blackened hole in the chest plate. *If the only thing they're fighting in this place is Yashelia, what killed this man?*

I had never heard of any aeon using a firearm, but the deadly placement of the shot made me sure it had not been friendly fire. I knelt and retrieved the pistol from the fallen purifier's hip holster. The weapon felt heavy in my grip. I stuffed it into the pocket of my coat. Both hands on my shotgun, I scanned the dense foliage and billowing smoke for signs of others.

Thomas. I have to find him, and then we have to get out of here.

Shouting behind me made me turn. I looked down the barrel of my shotgun at a group of four purifiers as they approached the trunk of the tree in the clearing. They didn't seem to see me. With as quiet a footstep as I could manage, I eased my back toward Yashelia's thorny tree. My heartbeat quickened. I checked the network for an instant and found threads of illusion surrounding the minds of the purifiers. Despite the light ship above, the purifiers here did not appear to be winning.

I walked out from behind the tree, gun ready, but trusting the squad before me would be too wrapped up in their illusions to attack. If Yashelia's illusionist, the other woman I had seen in the swamp from my memory, was precise enough and intended them to see me, I could easily have been killed. One of the purifiers looked in my direction, face mask expressionless. Then he fell to his knees, dropping the rifle he had been holding.

Yashelia emerged from the smoke behind them as droplets of cold rain pattered on the branches and leaves all around. I stared as she approached the purifiers who stood paralyzed before her. I aimed at her with my shotgun, but I knew from what I had felt inside Yashelia's tree-mind, I did not need her blood to restore Rebecca. That was already done. If I found Thomas, that was all it would take.

The rogue aeon approached the helpless purifiers in the center of the clearing. As she came closer, I saw her sleeves were soaked with blood up to the elbows. The eternal wound over her eye flowed with golden ichor, and the liquid dripped onto the forest floor with every step. Her gore-covered fingers made claws. She reached for the neck of the nearest purifier.

My hands shook. "Stop." I stepped out into the clearing, keeping my weapon trained on Yashelia as best I could. "Don't hurt them."

She looked at me. Bright eyes gleamed in a blood-streaked face. With deliberate slowness, she reached out and seized the man by the throat. I squeezed the trigger of my shotgun. The weapon kicked into my shoulder with a roar and sent a spray of shot toward Yashelia. She snapped the purifier's neck and caught the blast with his body in the same motion. He hung in her grip. Blood trickled through tears in his armor.

Yashelia threw the body. The corpse hit me high along the chest. I pulled the shotgun's trigger again as the impact bowled me onto my back. The shotgun's sound burst in my ears, and the shot went into the smoke and treetops behind Yashelia. Raindrops fell upon my face. I scrambled free of the body, shoving it away with a mix of desperation and revulsion. I stood and found the other three purifiers lying at Yashelia's feet, crushed or torn or strangled in instants.

"Jethro," she said. "You violated my mind." She stalked over the bodies and advanced on me. I raised the shotgun. She batted the barrel to the side before I could fire. In the next instant, she tugged the weapon from my grip and tossed it away.

I stepped back and plunged into the network. There, my perception of time gave me more thoughts before she could kill me. Still, it would only be seconds. Once in the network, I detected only two other minds left in the forest. Thomas, I recognized, hidden by the path near the clearing, and a lilting sonic mind I did not recognize, approaching from a path opposite the fires the purifiers had started, probably Yashelia's illusionist. I drew back to myself. Inside my own mind, I raced to think of way to stop her.

I opened my eyes. "Wait!"

Her hand closed around my throat and cut off my airflow. My feet fell back apace. I glared into Yashelia's face as she shoved my back against the tree. Thorns pierced my coat and dug into my skin. She smiled at me, a single line of blood flowing from the wound over her eye and dripping ichor onto my chest.

"Maybe it's not time for you to die," she said. "I will clean you instead." I grimaced as her grip relaxed and let me breathe again. Her free hand flew to the top of my head and pressed down. "You will enjoy being a slave. A good replacement for Rain. Yes, child, a good replacement."

I reached up and tried to remove her fingers, prying with both hands. She shook her head. "Do not fight. It will all be over soon."

I lashed out with a kick at her leg. I might as well have kicked an iron bar. I grunted in pain.

She smiled wider and wider, lips running with ichor. Then I saw no more reason to struggle. The only thought in my mind was that this beautiful creature, this lethal goddess was doing me a favor. All my worries could leave me. All this chaos could end. A simple way to be. It could be mine.

Then I tasted her kiss on my lips, covered with golden blood. Yashelia held my gaze with hers as she kissed me. Somehow, it all felt better now. I felt like my mind was falling asleep. Her kiss, the taste of her ichor, both were inhumanly sweet.

My eyelids began to flutter. On the dregs of the ichor newly fed into my system with her kiss, I entered the network instinctively.

A woman in the distance spoke, *"Jeth, don't give up. Jeth? Listen to me. She can't clean you as long as you don't have ichor in your system."*

Rebecca's voice sounded firm and human, not ethereal and sweet.

"But she's feeding me ichor right now."

"You have to fight. Thomas is on his way. We'll all be there soon."

"I can't fight. Not anymore."

"I left you, and I regretted it. Don't leave me now."

Those words I never expected to hear, like words from a teenage dream. I opened my eyes and looked at Yashelia, lips still pressed to mine. I spat her own ichor into her mouth. The aeon drew back and screamed. Her hand tightened once again on my throat, and she began to twist my head. I gritted my teeth. A gunshot rang out and made Yashelia turn. Thomas stood at the end of the path, pistol held in both hands.

I remembered the pistol I had retrieved from the fallen purifier and reached for it with a blind hand, mind blank except for the need to get the weapon. Yashelia turned toward Thomas slowly. I dragged the pistol from my coat pocket with a scratched and painful hand. I angled it upward and pulled the trigger.

The gun screamed, and a bullet cut through Yashelia's chest. She gave an animal roar and hurled me through the air. I hit Thomas like a flying rock, and we both went down. My spine ached, and I rolled off Thomas. I looked back at the tree. The light ship moved from overhead, dragging glowing lines, the purpose of which I did not understand, behind it. Falling rain doused the fires and reduced them to more smoke. Yashelia limped toward us from the place in the front of the tree where she had thrown me. Golden blood poured from the wound in her chest. A cloudiness fled from her eyes, making them look even brighter.

Thomas grunted and found his feet. I pushed myself up on hands and knees.

"We have to get moving," Thomas said and helped me stand.

I half-laughed, half-groaned. "No kidding."

He put an arm around my sides and dragged me after him, moving down the path. I looked back as Yashelia turned her back on us and struggled toward her tree. Her voice whispered after me on the network. *"Look after Rebecca, Jethro."* She sounded resigned and exhausted.

Thomas scowled. "Why is she letting us go?"

"I think she's tired." I glanced back at the tree. The fire hadn't touched it, but blood splashed across the trunk, and smoke darkened the branches. "We're lucky to get away."

I put my head down, and we kept walking.

Thomas and I emerged from the park, smoke billowing to the sky behind us and cold rain falling all around. Thomas' van stood at the street corner before us. The side door slid open, and Rebecca waved us inside. We didn't hesitate.

As I climbed into the van her hand touched my shoulder. I met her eyes and smiled despite the bloodshed left behind in the park. The expression on her face more than matched mine. The door slammed behind me, and we sped off.

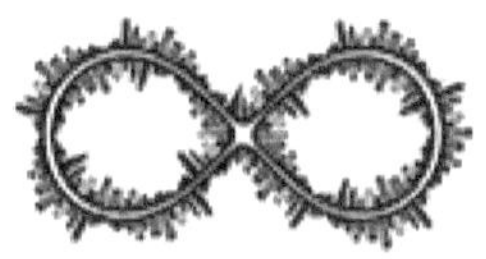

12

THREE DAYS LATER, I still ached all over and my cuts were only just healing. Accessing a healing link would be too suspicious given the circumstances. Instead, I hid my cuts and scrapes under layers of clothes and left my apartment to meet Rebecca, Elizabeth, and Thomas for breakfast. Everyone but Rebecca was worse for wear after the chaos of that evening.

The women filled me in about how Rebecca had awakened. I couldn't tell if she was happy or not at the result, but I didn't let myself worry about it. Thomas suggested, once we could get papers for her, we should find Rebecca an apartment in a different building in the district.

She glanced at me for a moment, then gave a small smile and told Thomas she liked the idea. After what had happened with Yashelia, and what she had said to me while we fled, I only had a moment's hesitation before I agreed. I figured if I wanted to be with Rebecca, I would have to give her some space first.

A network message from Omasoa called me in to review some text packets for distribution to a production team. Reluctantly, I sent back that I'd be right there. I saw Ryan Carter on the train to work. He crossed the compartment and sat down next to me, a metal flask in his hand. I could only assume it held ichor.

"You're better with a gun than you ever said."

I frowned at him. "I don't know what you mean."

"I mean I saw you. And Fenstein. In that garden."

"How?"

He tapped the side of his head, and then wiggled the flask. "I worked analysis for the op. Don't worry. I wanted to share some things with you."

I looked out the train windows at the rooftops flying past. "Thanks."

"Don't mention it. A lot of good people died out there, and I want to know why."

"You still don't?"

Ryan shook his head. "A mad aeon and some kind of illusionist were too much for purifiers without power suits or military support. Sudhatho must have known that when he sent them in because they were the distraction he used to seal the garden."

"That light ship," I murmured. "It was his."

"Right. And if Sudhatho knew they couldn't win, he sacrificed them deliberately." He scowled. "Let me show you what I know." He held out the flask, but I shook my head. I was already on my dose of ichor for the day.

I took a deep breath, and he reached out and gave me some memories he had found, the heavyset sensocycler, the purifier officer, and the furious battle he had seen from all sorts of angles. When the images and sounds subsided, I gasped for air. He put a hand on my shoulder.

When I recovered a little, I turned toward him. "Let's get to the bottom of this."

"We have to do it right," said Ryan. "The aeons might not be supportive of what we need to do."

"Yeah. Sudhatho is one of their own," I said. "So, that's probably an understatement."

We talked a little about other things, though I don't remember any of the subjects clearly. It didn't matter, because though the sky looked darker through the week, there hadn't been rain in three days. And when I got back to the tower that night, Elizabeth and I had a network to set up.

UNREGISTERED MEMORY, Ryan Carter, Security Analytics Offices, Marlowe Square

He sat with a cup of ichor before him on the table. Whenever Ryan thought of the forest, and the great tree he had made out in the chaos of the failed attack he couldn't help but shiver. All that mental power pent up and inaccessible by humans except when someone touched it. He exhaled slowly, trying to calm his mind. A sigh came out in place of normal breath. *What does someone do with that much power?*

"Plenty of time to find out," he said to himself, then checked over his new contacts. Alesia De Vries' and Conner Kohl's mental signatures drifted in his mind. He sipped his ichor, then leaned back and closed his eyes. A small smile worked its way onto his face, then he shot off into the mental city.

I RETURNED HOME TO Lotdel tower that night and found Elizabeth waiting in the lobby. She stood up from the chair, where she had been sitting, and met me in the center of the mostly vacant room.

"What's wrong?" I asked.

Elizabeth shrugged. "I just wanted to talk to you."

"Can't we talk upstairs?" I said.

She shook her head. "Rebecca's up there. The bureau didn't accept her new papers."

I frowned. "I guess it can't be helped. We'll have to find a better set of those to get her registered. Don't worry, I'll take care of that as soon as I can."

"Do you want her to stay with you until then?"

My eyebrows rose. "Is that what this is about? I don't see how I could. Nageddia might start asking questions if I did."

Elizabeth looked down at her folded hands. "I talked to Thomas. She can stay in the Mangrove Suite for now."

"Thanks." I remembered the memories she had shared with me from the past few days and put a hand on her shoulder. "For everything you've done."

She shrugged off my hand and walked back to the elevator. She hit the call button. I looked at her with her hair shining under the light veins set in the ceiling. Elizabeth looked over her shoulder at me. "Come on, Jeth. We've got work to do."

I smiled at her and followed her to the elevator. The doors opened, and we went inside. As we rode upward, I couldn't help but ask myself a question that made me uncomfortable. Why had Yashelia wanted Rain so badly? I sighed as I realized, even if Rebecca knew, she might never want to tell me. Elizabeth and I stopped at the level of our apartments.

We were about to part when I turned to her. "You ready to set up our news network?"

"Not tonight." Elizabeth put a hand on my arm. "For now, I just want to rest." She slipped away, for once light to the touch. Something had changed between us, but I didn't understand what, even with the memories she had lent me.

I walked home, turning thoughts over and over in my mind even as my day's dose of ichor ran out. I remembered the illusions I had seen in Yashelia's garden, and the flooded woods of my childhood. I took a deep breath. The water began to rise once again.

AN END

THANKS FOR READING the Mangrove Suite!

Jeth and his friends return in book two "The Cleanway" Available at the link below:

https://www.amazon.com/dp/B0795993Z3

ABOUT THE AUTHOR

I'm Tim Niederriter. As you've no doubt gathered, I write books of science fiction, fantasy, and combinations of the two for fun and novelty.

I'm the son of two physicists from Pennsylvania, transplanted to Minnesota. My parents read me the Hobbit (repeatedly) at a young age. The math adds up. I love both far-flung science fiction and epic fantasy of all kinds.

Diagnosed with an autism spectrum disorder at a young age, I've always surrounded myself with fictional worlds. I studied writing and literature at Gustavus Adolphus College and have a strong interest in history and politics as well.

I co-host the roleplaying game podcast "Of Mooks and Monsters" and talk with other authors each week on my other podcast, "Alive After Reading."